Usborne

Illustrated Stories from Dickens

Usborne

Illustrated Stories from Dickens

Adapted by
Mary Sebag-Montefiore

Illustrated by Barry Ablett

Contents

Oliver Twist

Contents

Chapter 1

Nobody's baby

"Take… care… of… him." The young mother's whisper was as soft as the swirling snow outside; her face as white as the sheet that covered her. Feebly she touched her newborn son, breathed a last sigh, and closed her eyes.

"She's dead!" announced Mrs. Mann, the midwife. "What a nuisance. I'll have to get Mr. Bumble."

Mr. Bumble was in charge of the workhouse – a cold, grim place for the homeless, without a spark of comfort or a crumb of nourishing food. He didn't care if the inmates starved, as long as his own tummy felt warm and full three times a day.

Quickly, Mrs. Mann unclasped a gold locket from the dead woman's neck and put it around her own. Opening it, she read the name "Agnes" engraved inside.

"Another orphan brat," raged Mr. Bumble, when he saw the baby. "Who is he anyway?"

"Who knows?" Mrs. Mann yawned. "His mother walked in yesterday off the street. She must have walked some distance – her shoes were worn out. Good-looking girl, too."

"He must have a name..." Mr. Bumble thought hard. "Well, I name all orphans alphabetically and the last one was Smith, so he can be Twist. Oliver Twist."

"Ooh, Mr. Bumble, you are clever," smiled Mrs. Mann, fluttering her eyelashes at him. She wrapped Oliver in a scrap of cloth, yellowed with age.

Oliver opened his mouth and roared with all the force of his baby lungs. If he'd understood he was an orphan, loved by no one, he would have cried even louder.

Chapter 2

More means less

By the time Oliver was seven he was sleeping in a dormitory with fifty other starving boys.

"I'm so hungry I could eat the boy in the next bed!" complained a tall, strong boy with wild, angry eyes.

The boy in the next bed gulped. "We must have more food," he agreed, hastily. "Let's draw straws to decide who's going to ask Mr. Bumble."

Oliver's heart was thumping as he reached out to draw his straw. He pulled it close. "Oh no!" he cried. "It's me."

Supper, as usual, was gruel – a kind of thin watery porridge with a few lumps of gristle floating in it. The boys lined up in front of Mr. Bumble who stood at one end of the dining room, a huge apron tied around his fat belly, ladling a small spoonful into each boy's bowl.

They returned to their tables to eat their food, packed on benches as tight as sardines, though not so plump. Their bowls never needed washing.

They were licked clean in seconds until they shone like polished china.

The boys sitting near Oliver kicked him under the table.

"Go on, Oliver."

"Ask NOW."

Shivering with fear, Oliver walked the length of the room. He clutched his bowl so tightly, his knuckles gleamed white.

A terrible silence descended, pierced by Oliver's slow echoing footsteps on the stone floor. He passed table after table of boys, their spoons laid down, their empty bowls in front of them. Each round-eyed boy stared at him expectantly as he went by. Oliver guessed what they were thinking – *I'm glad it's him, not me.* At last he reached Mr. Bumble, who looked down his nose at Oliver, as though he were an insect he wanted to squash.

Oliver forced himself to speak. "Please sir, I want some more," he whispered.

"WHAT?" shouted Mr. Bumble.

"Please sir, I want some more."

Mr. Bumble swelled like an evil giant. His eyes bulged with fury and his face went purple. "More? How DARE you! Wicked boy!"

He seized Oliver, hit him with the gruel ladle and threw him into the coal cellar, locking the door. "Your punishment starts here," he bellowed.

Oliver heard him stump up the steps, muttering as he went. "No one's ever asked for more before. Mark my words, he'll be a criminal when he grows up. That boy will hang!"

In the dark, sooty cellar, cobwebs stroked
Oliver's face like creepy fingers, and rats
scratched the walls. He crouched in a corner,
pressing himself close to the wall. Its hard,
cold surface felt almost protective in the lonely
gloom. He stayed awake all night, dreading
what would happen to him next.

Chapter 3

Running away

As Oliver crouched in the cellar, Mr. Bumble was nailing an advertisement to the workhouse door.

The next day, Mr. Bumble dragged Oliver
from the cellar. "There are two men coming to
see you," he said, "so make sure you behave."

Oliver watched as the first man pulled up
outside the door, in a donkey cart laden with
soot.

"Whoah!" he shouted, hitting the donkey on
the head with a great thump from his whip.

"Mr. Gamfield," said Mr. Bumble, stepping
out to greet him.

Mr. Gamfield stared at Oliver. "He's a very *small* boy. But I need an apprentice to climb chimneys and sweep out soot. Some of the chimneys are narrow and twisting. This brat will fit nicely."

"I won't go with him! I won't!" cried Oliver.

"Don't be so insolent," said Mr. Bumble.

"I've heard about chimney sweeps," Oliver said. "You can die up a chimney. They light a fire to make you hurry down, and you get smothered in the smoke."

"Nonsense!" said Mr. Gamfield. "I just gets a nice crackling blaze going and the boys come down quicker than anything."

"Then I'll frizzle in flames. I'm not going," replied Oliver firmly.

Mr. Gamfield clambered back into his donkey cart. "I don't want a rebellious boy. You've spoiled him, Mr. Bumble."

With that, he whipped the donkey until it trotted away.

Mr. Bumble shook Oliver until his teeth rattled. "Keep your mouth shut or no one will want you," he bellowed. "You've ruined that chance. Don't ruin the next. Look! Here it comes now."

He pointed to a thin, spidery man coming up to the door.

The man had a gloomy air. "I am Mr. Sowerberry," he introduced himself. "I arrange funerals and I need help." He looked at Oliver closely. "This boy will do, but he's so thin, he's not worth five pounds. I'll give you three pounds for him. Take it or leave it."

Mr. Bumble was disgusted, but there was nothing he could do. He was eager to see the last of Oliver. "Glad you're going, Oliver. Behave, or else..." he threatencd.

Back at his shop, Mr. Sowerberry showed Oliver a dusty basement. A dim light filtered in, through a grimy pane of glass barred with rusty iron rails.

"You'll sleep here, you little bag of bones," he said.

Oliver looked around the shadowy room. It was stacked with empty coffins and planks of wood. Drapes of black cloth hung from hooks in the walls, billowing occasionally in the breeze, as though first they breathed... and then were lifeless. The only place to sleep – a recess behind the coffins where a thin mattress was thrust – looked like a grave.

"And this is Noah, my apprentice," Mr. Sowerberry went on, taking him to the kitchen. "Noah, give Oliver his supper."

Noah looked cross. "What work is he going to do?" he asked, sulkily.

"He'll be a mute. He's a good-looking boy. Dressed in a top hat and mourning clothes, he'll be a credit to the business."

"Please sir, what's a mute?" asked Oliver.

"A mute walks next to the coffin at funerals and follows it to the grave. Children's funerals only. Winter's coming on – always lots of children's funerals this time of year..."

Noah grinned unpleasantly when Mr. Sowerberry left them alone. "Here's your food." He handed Oliver the dog's bowl.

Oliver was so hungry, he wolfed down the stinking scraps of fat that even the dog had left.

"Pig!" mocked Noah. "Workhouse Boy! If your mother hadn't died, she'd be in prison. She must have been bad. Only bad 'uns give birth in the workhouse."

"Don't you dare say anything against my mother!" shouted Oliver.

"So? What are you going to do about it?" Noah jeered.

"This!" Oliver punched Noah hard in his flabby stomach. Noah collapsed like a crumpled balloon.

"Ow!" he squealed. "HELP! MURDER!
Mr. Sowerberry? You've lost your mind,
Oliver Twist. You just wait, Workhouse Boy.
You'll be punished for this."

"Do what you want," replied Oliver.
"I'm not staying here any longer." He raced
out of the door and tore down the road, his
heart pounding. "Don't let them come after
me," he prayed.

LONDON
70 MILES

Chapter 4

New friends

Oliver ran and ran until he came to a signpost. "I'll walk to London," he decided. "Perhaps I can make a better life for myself there."

He walked ten miles a day. At night he hid in hay barns and woke each morning aching and weak with hunger. The nights were worst, because there was nothing around him but darkness and loneliness.

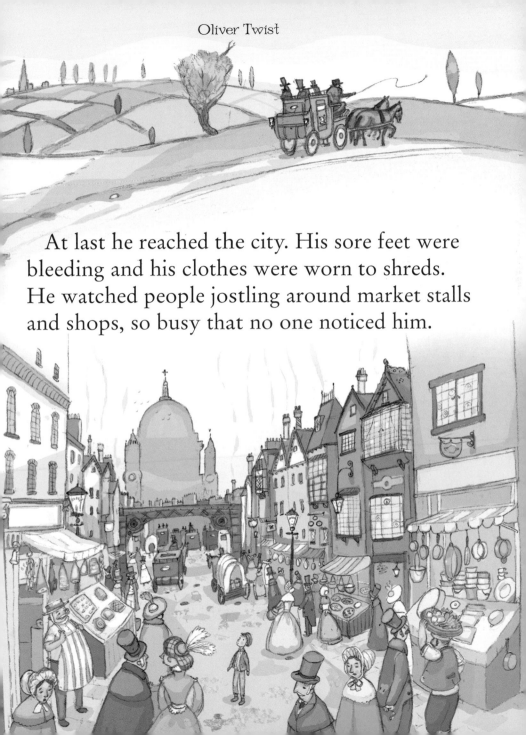

At last he reached the city. His sore feet were bleeding and his clothes were worn to shreds. He watched people jostling around market stalls and shops, so busy that no one noticed him.

He collapsed on a cold doorstep, too exhausted to beg. Delicious smells floated by from a bakery. Oliver staggered up to the window, where shelves groaned with piles of freshly-made bread, cakes, buns and pies. He stared at them longingly.

A boy about the same age, with sharp eyes and a swaggering walk, strolled over. "Hungry?" he asked.

"Very," gasped Oliver.

To Oliver's astonishment, the boy pulled a wad of money out of his pocket.

"I'll get you something. Wait here."

The boy returned with a bag crammed with hot meat pies.

"I'm Dodger," said the boy, as Oliver gobbled the food. "You?"

"Oliver Twist."

"Got a bed tonight, Oliver?"

"No."

"Got any family?"

"No one at all."

"I know a kind gentleman who'll take you in. He won't want any rent, either."

"That's generous!" exclaimed Oliver. He followed Dodger down a maze of narrow alleys, where foul smells filled the air and swarms of ragged urchins played in slimy, oozing gutters. Men and women staggered around, cursing.

It looked so dirty, Oliver almost wished he hadn't come, but he had nowhere else to go. Finally, they reached a crumbling house. Dodger led him up a rickety staircase to a dark room.

Through a cloud of sizzling fumes, Oliver spied a gnarled old man. He was wearing a grubby blue coat and frying sausages over the fire.

Behind him, a group of boys danced and dodged, playing a game. The old man's coat had lots of pockets, stuffed with hankies, wallets and pens and the boys were trying to pull them out without him noticing.

"Hey, Fagin," yelled Dodger. "This is Oliver."

"Hello, Oliver." Fagin bared his teeth in a leering grin. "Want to play?"

"Yes sir," said Oliver politely. He waited until Fagin bent over the frying pan, crept up… and delicately drew out a hanky.

"You're a natural!" chuckled Fagin. "Come near the fire. Have a sausage!"

Another man stepped in, smearing the back of his dirty hand across his mouth. With him were a girl and a snarling dog with a scratched, torn face.

"Ah, Bill Sikes," drawled Fagin. "Delighted to see you! What can I do for you and Nancy?"

"Give Bullseye supper," Bill growled, kicking his dog. "And get me a drink."

"Get to work, boys," Fagin ordered. One found a bone for the dog, while Dodger gave Nancy a half-full jug of gin. She emptied it into a brimming mug and passed it to Bill.

"Bill's scary," Oliver thought, snuggling under his blanket that night. "But I'm lucky to have found new friends."

The next morning, waking in the pale
half-light of dawn, Oliver saw Fagin open
a chest and run his hands over necklaces,
sparkling rings and shining gold coins.

Fagin turned to face Oliver's gaze. He thrust
the chest back under the floor, seized a knife
and pressed the blade into Oliver's neck.

"What did you see?"
he hissed.

"Nothing,"
stammered Oliver,
terrified.

"Good boy," said Fagin, letting go. "Keep quiet, or you'll be sorry. That's all I have to keep me in my old age. Do what you're told, Oliver, if you want to be happy here."

A few days later, Fagin told Oliver to go out with Dodger. They stopped by a bookshop which had a stall outside in the street. A richly-dressed gentleman had picked up a book from the stall and was reading it as hard as if he was in his study.

"See him?" asked Dodger. "Prime target. Stick by me."

With one slick move, Dodger pulled a wallet from the gentleman's coat pocket.

In that moment, Oliver saw what his new friends were. Thieves!

Chapter 5

Betrayed

The gentleman spun around, realizing he'd been robbed. "STOP THIEF!" he yelled at Oliver.

Oliver looked for Dodger but he'd vanished. Panicking, Oliver raced off, followed by every man and woman in the street.

"STOP THIEF!" they shouted, chasing him helter-skelter through mud and puddles, throwing sticks and stones at his scrawny back.

Oliver, breathless, kept running until a stone struck his head. He fell down, stunned. "Please sir," he whispered, as the gentleman reached him. "I'm not a thief."

The gentleman stared at him. "Hmm... Well, you look honest. Indeed, you look like–" He stopped, puzzled. "I'm sure I know that face," he murmured.

"Get the police," said a passer-by.

"No. He deserves a chance," replied the gentleman. "Who are you, boy? My name's Brownlow. Perhaps I can help you. Come with me."

Mr. Brownlow took Oliver to his grand house. In the hallway was a portrait of a beautiful girl. Oliver stopped and stared at it, drinking it in.

"That was my niece, Agnes," said Mr. Brownlow. "She had a sad life. I wish she'd come to me for help. She must be dead now, poor girl." He looked at the portrait, then at Oliver. "I can't believe it," he muttered. "The likeness is extraordinary... Where were you born?" he asked urgently.

"In Mr. Bumble's workhouse," Oliver replied, surprised at the sudden question.

"Yes, I've heard of it," said Mr. Brownlow, nodding and looking grim. "Now, tell me about yourself."

Oliver recounted his life story, up until the moment he ran from the bookshop.

"I believe you," said Mr. Brownlow. He put his hands on Oliver's shoulders and looked down at him. "Would you like to live here and go to school?"

"Really?" gasped Oliver. "Truly?"

Mr. Brownlow laughed. "I'll have Mrs. Bedwin, my housekeeper, show you to your room."

"You poor child," sighed Mrs. Bedwin, as she took Oliver upstairs. "So dirty and ragged. Have a hot bath and I'll get you some clean clothes."

Lying in bed that night Oliver had never felt happier. And, as the weeks passed, he grew happier still. Mrs. Bedwin looked after him, from a good breakfast each morning to a hug last thing at night. Mr. Brownlow played games with him, shared his books and taught him chess and music.

44

"I feel as if I'm living in a dream," thought Oliver.

A few weeks later, Mr. Brownlow summoned him to his study. "Here's five pounds and some books. Will you take them to the bookshop where we met?"

"Of course," replied Oliver. "I'll do anything for you!"

"And come straight home," Mr. Brownlow added.

"I'll run there and back again," Oliver promised. He ran down the front steps and waved goodbye to Mrs. Bedwin, who was watching him from the window.

"Bless him," she thought. "I can't bear to let him out of my sight."

46

Oliver whistled as he strolled down the street. Suddenly, a pair of arms seized him tightly around the neck.

"OW!" he yelled. "Let go."

"Oh, Oliver, you naughty boy! I've found you at last."

Oliver was astonished. It was Nancy, Bill Sikes' friend. "Nancy – is that you? What are you doing here?"

A crowd gathered, staring at them.

"He's my little runaway brother," Nancy announced in a silky, false voice.

"But…" Oliver began.

Bill Sikes shot out of a beer shop with his snarling dog and grabbed Oliver.

"Watch him, Bullseye," he hissed.

Bullseye seized Oliver's leg and hung on to it with his sharp teeth.

"I don't belong to these people!" shouted Oliver, struggling to get away. "I have to go back to Mr. Brownlow."

But Nancy quickly covered his mouth until he nearly suffocated.

Bill dragged him through the alleyways, Bullseye growling at Oliver's every step, until they reached Fagin's attic.

"Good of you to drop in, Oliver," drawled Fagin sarcastically.

"Fancy clothes," laughed Dodger.

"Expensive books! We'll sell everything," crowed Fagin. He examined Oliver's pockets. "Aha! Even better. Here's five pounds."

"Mine," growled Bill.

"No, mine, surely," contradicted Fagin, but Bill snatched it away.

"It's Mr. Brownlow's," said Oliver bitterly.
"Let me go," he begged. "Or Mr. Brownlow
will think I'm a thief."

Fagin patted his head. "We'll make you
one soon."

"NO!" Oliver shouted. "Why do you
want me anyway?"

"So you can't tell tales," sneered Bill. "Once
you're one of us, you won't dare tell the
police. Now shut up."

Chapter 6

A robbery

Oliver was forced to wear filthy rags again. For several days the thieves made him stay in the attic, watched over by the vicious Bullseye.

Every time Oliver went near the door, Bullseye snarled, showing his sharp fangs.

"Don't set the dog on him, Bill," Nancy begged. "You've got Oliver back. You don't have to frighten him now."

"Oh don't I?" snarled Bill. He brandished a pistol. "See this, Oliver?"

Oliver nodded nervously.

"It's loaded. If you don't do what you're told, I'll fire. Understand?"

"Yes, Bill," said Oliver, trembling.

"Good. There's a job I want to do tonight. Big house, loaded with silver and jewels. They keep a small window open and I need a scrap of a boy to slip through it and undo the locks on the door."

"He means what he says about the gun," advised Fagin. "Don't try and cross Bill Sikes."

When night fell, Bill dragged Oliver to the house. They hid under a bush until the church clock struck midnight. It was intensely dark.

Bill hoisted Oliver up to a tiny window. "Get in," he hissed.

"Please don't make me steal," implored Oliver.

Sikes raised his fist. "Do it, or I'll bash your head in."

He shoved Oliver through the window, lit a lantern and handed it to him. "Open the front door," he ordered. "There's a bolt at the top you won't reach, so stand on one of the chairs. Remember, you're in my gunshot range."

Oliver saw Bill's pistol aimed at him. He had no choice: he crept inside and went to unlock the door.

As he slid back the bolt, he heard Bill running around to the front of the house.

"I must warn the family, somehow," Oliver thought. "I don't care what happens to me." And he dropped the lantern with a clatter.

After that, everything seemed to happen at once. Bill burst in to grab Oliver, a man appeared with a gun, and both men fired.

Oliver screamed, caught in the crossfire. He clutched his arm and saw his sleeve turn red.

Bill dragged him outside. "You fool," he growled. "They'll be after us. RUN!"

But Oliver, his arm throbbing, lagged behind. Bill flung him into a ditch. "You're too slow," he yelled down at him. "You can die here."

When Bill finally reached Fagin's house, Nancy rushed up to him. "How did it go?" she asked.

"Disaster," said Bill curtly. "Get me a drink."

"Where's the boy, Bill?"

"Dying in a ditch somewhere."

"You can't leave him there," Nancy cried. "I'll go and find him."

Bill lurched to his feet. "Don't you dare, Nancy!" But Nancy had already grabbed her cloak and was running through the door. A crafty look spread over Bill's face.

"After her, Bullseye," he ordered. "She won't get away with this."

Nancy ran to the house Bill had tried to rob and searched everywhere for Oliver. At last she found him, weak and shivering.

"Thank you for coming," he muttered.
She quickly bandaged his bleeding arm with her shawl. "I found your friend Mr. Brownlow. I'll take you to him," she whispered. "He'll be waiting for us on London Bridge."

"I don't believe you," Oliver said. "It's a trick."

"It isn't, Oliver, I promise. I met Mr. Brownlow yesterday. It's all arranged."

"Why are you doing this?"

"I've worked for Fagin since I was little. I don't want you to suffer like me."

"Stay with me," Oliver urged her. "Mr. Brownlow will look after you too. We could both start a new life."

"I can't leave Bill," Nancy shrugged. "I know he's bad, but I love him. Besides," she added, "I've been a thief all my life. It's too late to change now."

"It's never too late," said Oliver.

They hurried through the dark streets where flickering gas lamps shone eerie shafts of light on the cobbles.

Neither of them saw the dog following them – a dog with a scratched torn face and an eager snarling mouth. And behind the dog, a man, who moved with silent, stealthy footsteps through the shadows.

Chapter 7

The secret of the locket

They reached the bridge at dawn. Mr. Brownlow was waiting, just as Nancy had promised. "Run!" she cried to Oliver. Oliver dashed forward. He'd almost reached Mr. Brownlow's outstretched arms when Nancy's frightened voice made him turn around.

"W-why did you follow me, Bill?" Nancy stuttered. "I told no tales – I'd never grass on you."

"You took the boy away," Bill bellowed. "You betrayed me, Nancy. I can't ever trust you again."

Then Oliver heard Nancy scream. "No! Please, Bill, NO!"

BANG! A pistol shot exploded and Nancy slumped lifeless to the ground. Bill swore and closed his eyes. "I had to kill her," he muttered.

Oliver was frozen to the spot with terror.

"I'm here, Oliver," said Mr. Brownlow, reassuringly. "Come to me. Don't look."

By now, a crowd had appeared, drawn by the sound of the pistol shot. Bill fled from the bridge, desperate to escape.

The crowd tore after him. In a panic, Bill climbed the drainpipe of a nearby house and scaled the roof.

He grabbed a rope that was dangling from its chimney, intending to swing over to the roof of the house opposite. Quickly, he made a loop and slipped it over his head.

But before he could bring it down his body and under his arms, a policeman sounded his whistle below.

"Stop him!" cried a woman. "He's getting away."

Bill lost his balance and tumbled off the roof, the rope tightening around his neck. In seconds, he was dead, his body swaying in mid-air.

Bullseye ran back and forth, howling dismally. Then the dog leaped at the dead man, trying to reach him. Instead, he dashed his head on a stone windowsill and fell to the ground. The dog was as dead as his master.

Mr. Brownlow held Oliver firmly in his arms. Oliver couldn't stop shaking.

"Nothing can hurt you now," Mr. Brownlow told him. "You're safe. Bill deserved that, for what he did to Nancy."

"Poor Nancy," Oliver sobbed.

"Yes, she was a brave girl." He hugged Oliver tightly. "Listen, Oliver, I have good news for both of us. I went to see Mr. Bumble and he gave me this." He handed Oliver a gold locket. "Open it."

Oliver looked at the inscription inside. "Agnes," he read.

"Mrs. Mann, the midwife who was with your mother at the workhouse, stole this locket from her.

Later, Mrs. Mann married Mr. Bumble. That's how he discovered the locket."

"Was Agnes my mother?" Oliver asked.

"Yes. Your mother and my niece. I gave her the locket many years ago – I recognized it at once. You remember her portrait at home? You look just like her."

Mr. Brownlow hugged Oliver again. "You're my boy now," he said.

"Do I really belong to you?" Oliver asked, hardly daring to believe it.

Mr. Brownlow smiled. "You really do. Please God, your unhappy life is over forever. Let's go, Oliver. Mrs. Bedwin is longing to see you again."

And, hand-in-hand, they walked home.

Bleak House

Contents

Chapter 1

The plots begin

Fog. It choked your throat; it hid the shops; it veiled the river. It swirled all over London. It seemed that the sun was dead, and all that was left was the fog and dirt of cold, cruel November.

In the very heart of the fog was Lincoln's Inn Hall. Deep inside the Hall sat the Lord High Chancellor in his wig and gown. All around him lawyers droned on, in the case of *Jarndyce and Jarndyce*. It was about a Will.

Long ago, Mr. Jarndyce had died and left a fortune, but no immediate heir. His cousins had fought for the money in court. Their children and their children's children had fought for it. Lawyers had argued about it for decades. The case of *Jarndyce* stank of trickery and delay. It was as murky as the misty cloak hanging over London.

Far away, in a grand country house, Mr. Tulkinghorn, a family lawyer, had come to see Sir Leicester and Lady Dedlock about that very case.

"If you sign this paper, Lady Dedlock," he said, "it will help your claim."

"But it's so dull," drawled Lady Dedlock, looking bored. "Will *Jarndyce* never end?"

Sir Leicester smiled indulgently. After all their years of marriage, he still adored her.

Lady Dedlock took the piece of paper and her face turned deathly white. "Who... who wrote this?" she stammered, and she slumped to the ground.

"My dear, what's the matter?" Sir Leicester was at her side in an instant.

"I'm fine," she muttered, as she came to. "I just felt faint for a moment."

Mr. Tulkinghorn narrowed his eyes, thinking quickly. Had Lady Dedlock recognized the handwriting? Is that why she 'felt faint'? Perhaps there was an opportunity here for blackmail. He bowed to Sir Leicester and left the room.

As he crossed the hall, he heard a woman snarling like a tigress, "How I hate Lady Dedlock! Now she humiliates me!"

"Who are you?" he asked.

"Je suis Hortense," hissed the woman. "Her French maid. She is going to replace me with a village girl. How dare she!"

"I'm sure no one could replace you, Hortense," said Mr. Tulkinghorn. If he could get her on his side, she might help him. "Here is my address," he went on. "I will pay you for any information about Lady Dedlock."

His lips stretched in a sinister smile. "After all, it is my duty as the family lawyer to protect Sir Leicester."

"Of course," said Hortense, grinning. She guessed he was lying, but she liked the thought of easy money. "I will be your spy."

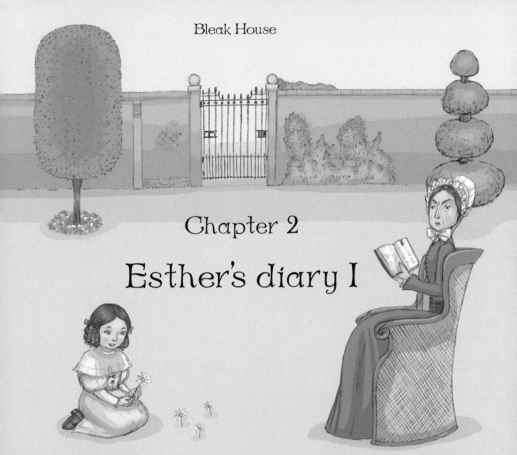

Chapter 2

Esther's diary I

My name is Esther Summerson. All my life I've felt like an outsider. I've never met my parents, I don't even know their names. I was brought up by my godmother, Miss Barbary. Once when I begged her to tell me where I came from, she replied, "Your mother, Esther, is your disgrace, as you are hers. You are set apart. You have no family."

When I was still quite a young woman, Miss Barbary fell ill suddenly and died. I was left with no one. Then, the day after her burial, her lawyer Mr. Guppy arrived with surprising news.

"My client, Mr. Jarndyce, knew Miss Barbary," he told me. "He promised to be your guardian and is inviting you to live with him at Bleak House."

"How wonderful," I gasped in relief. I'd been so worried. At least I wasn't homeless.

Mr. Guppy always stares at me. I think he likes me, but he makes me feel uncomfortable.

Bleak House is huge and grand, beaming with
light. And Mr. Jarndyce is so kind, like the father
I'd never had. When I arrived he opened his arms
wide, and said, "Welcome. You are home." Home!
It's such a lovely word.

Two other young people live at Bleak House:
Richard and Ada. They are cousins, claimants in the
Jarndyce case, like Mr. Jarndyce himself, and both
orphans like me. Mr. Jarndyce looks after us all.

"Let's be sisters," Ada said to me gleefully. It made me so happy... as if I belonged. Richard is handsome and fun, though restless. First he wanted to be a sailor; now he's training to be a soldier. He joked, "If I win the Jarndyce case, I'll be so rich I'll never work." Silly Richard! Surely it's enough to have a home and be content.

When we were walking in the woods, Mr. Jarndyce said, "Little Woman," – that's become his nickname for me – "if there's anything you want, please tell me." I confided my greatest wish, that I longed to know my background. In my dreams I find my mother... and she strokes my hair.

"I only know this," said Mr. Jarndyce. "Your godmother asked me to be your guardian after her death. She said such cruel words about the shame of your existence that I felt sorry for you. I want you to be happy."

As he spoke, a beautiful lady strolled into view. Mr. Jarndyce introduced us. "Lady Dedlock, who lives nearby. Miss Esther Summerson."

Her proud eyes held mine for a moment. In that short time, though I had never seen her before, I knew her face well. She looked like Miss Barbary, though not so cross. She looked – it was so strange – like me.

Chapter 3

The handwriting

Mr. Tulkinghorn went all over Lincoln's Inn, in and out of the offices where men sat writing legal documents. He held the paper that had caused Lady Dedlock's collapse before each of them.

"Do you know this handwriting?" he asked in every office.

At last he found the answer.

"That's Nemo's," said a clerk. "He lives opposite, above Krook's Rag-and-Bottle shop."

"Nemo?" muttered Mr. Tulkinghorn. "But that's Latin for no one..."

The Rag-and-Bottle shop window was crammed with shabby painted signs. Mr. Tulkinghorn pushed open the door. It creaked. Inside were stinking piles of dirty bottles that once held beer, wine, medicine and ink. Beyond them sat an old man and a cat by a dismal fire.

"Are you Krook?" Mr. Tulkinghorn inquired. "I'm looking for Nemo."

"He's upstairs, miserable as usual I expect," Krook grunted. "Take a candle."

Mr. Tulkinghorn climbed into a filthy, empty room. A man with matted hair and bare feet lay on the floor. His skin had a yellow look and a bitter smell hung in the air.

When Mr. Tulkinghorne shook him, there was no response – no breath in the nostrils, no warmth in the body. The man was dead.

Mr. Tulkinghorn searched the room and found a packet of letters tied with a ribbon. He snatched them up and hid them in his coat pocket. Then he went back downstairs.

A thin ragged boy, who looked as if he'd never had a bath in his life, had crept into the shop.

"He's dead," Tulkinghorn said abruptly to Krook. "An overdose, I suppose. Who was he?"

Krook shrugged. "I think he was a soldier once. But he lost all his money."

"Did anyone know him?"

"I did," said the boy.

"And you are?" asked Mr. Tulkinghorn.

"Jo," Krook said. "Ain't got no other name. Can't even read. He's a beggar."

Jo turned to Mr. Tulkinghorn. "It's not true! I earn my bread! I sweep horse muck off the streets. Nemo gave me money when he could. He was good to me."

"Ugh!" shuddered Mr. Tulkinghorn, heading for the door. "Just keep away from me, you filthy child."

Mr. Tulkinghorn hurried home to inspect his find. They were passionate love letters, all written to a Captain Hawdon and signed: Honoria Barbary. The letters told the story of a love affair, of a baby born to Honoria, young, unmarried, and now dreading disgrace in the eyes of society. The baby died. The affair finished.

As the Dedlock family lawyer, Mr. Tulkinghorn knew that Honoria Barbary had married and was now... Lady Dedlock.

The very next day, he went to see the Dedlocks in their London house and asked to see Lady Dedlock alone.

"Why alone?" demanded Sir Leicester.

"I don't mind," said Lady Dedlock. "I'm sure it's nothing important."

As soon as Sir Leicester had left the room, Mr. Tulkinghorn turned on Lady Dedlock. "I know who wrote that document," he sneered.

"I'm not interested," said Lady Dedlock, haughtily, freezing her face into an arrogant mask.

"He's dead," Mr. Tulkinghorn went on. "But his name was Captain Hawdon, also known as Nemo. He lived over a shop in Lincoln's Inn and had no friends, except a beggar boy named Jo... And you."

"I have nothing to say."

"Really? I know all your secrets, Lady Dedlock. Your love affair. Your dead baby, born out of marriage. Your disgrace."

Mr. Tulkinghorn's voice was icy with dislike. "Sir Leicester is a proud man. He would never forgive you if your shame became public knowledge."

Lady Dedlock knew this was true. She trembled, though she tried to hide it.

Nothing escaped the lawyer's eyes. It thrilled him to see this haughty woman devastated by his words.

He bowed. "Goodbye, Lady Dedlock. Live with your guilt. One day I shall tell the world that the proud Lady Dedlock is a liar and a fraud."

That evening Sir Leicester asked her, "What did Tulkinghorn want to say to you so privately?"

For one desperate second, she hesitated. She wanted to tell him, but she could not. Fear struggled with honesty, and fear won.

"Nothing important," she said.

Chapter 4

Esther's diary II

I've met the doctor here. His name is Allan Woodcourt. We get along so well. We make each other laugh. He's young and handsome, not in the least like that lawyer, the smarmy Mr. Guppy. And he's thoughtful. He knows Lady Dedlock. He says her pride hides a tortured soul.

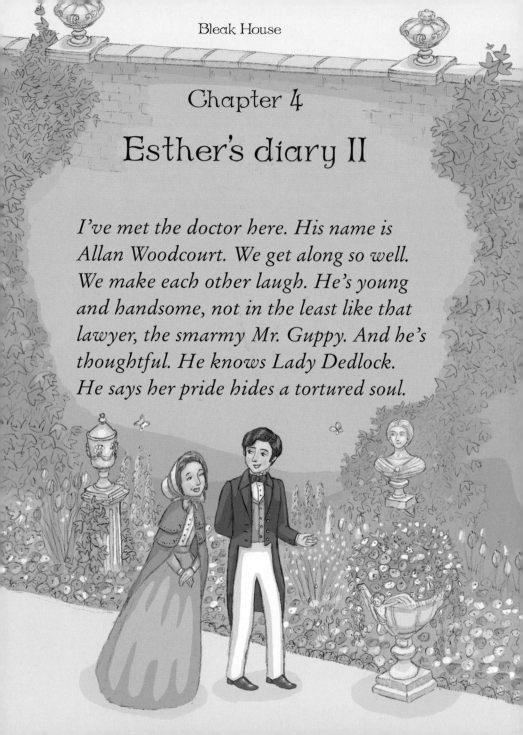

We all went, Mr. Jarndyce, Richard, Ada and I, to have tea with Allan's mother. She saw him look at me, and afterwards she took me aside: "I want Allan to marry someone of good family," she said. "We Woodcourts are very proud, you know." She meant, "Keep away from my son." She knows I'm an orphan – just a nobody. I wish I knew where I came from. Mr. Jarndyce noticed my unhappiness, and was extra kind to me.

Richard and Ada are falling in love. Richard is training to be a lawyer now, because he wants to win the Jarndyce case.

"Another career change!" Ada exclaimed. "Why bother with winning? I don't mind being poor."

Richard laughed at her. "I want to be rich!"

"All right," Ada sighed, her eyes huge with love. She can't see that Richard is neither intelligent nor steady. Mr. Jarndyce understands. He thinks it's the uncertainty of the Jarndyce case that has made Richard so indecisive and willing to take risks.

Mr. Guppy comes almost every day. He always says, "Oh Miss Summerson, you do look beautiful!" I'm polite, but I avoid him whenever possible. He's too grovelling.

I don't know why it is, I always seem to be writing about myself. I do mean to write about other people. I hope anyone who reads my diary understands I really don't want to concentrate on myself.

Chapter 5

A mystery solved

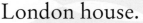

Mr. Guppy was so in love with Esther that he wanted to propose. "And I know how to win her heart," he thought. "I'll find her parents. It should be easy enough for a lawyer. Then she'll be so grateful, she'll have to marry me."

The startling discovery he made took him straight to Lady Dedlock in her London house.

"Do you know a Miss Esther Summerson?" he asked.

"I have met her," said Lady Dedlock.

"The person who brought her up was named Miss Barbary. She said she was Esther's godmother. In fact, she was her aunt – and your sister. Esther Summerson's real name is Esther Hawdon. Her father was a law writer, who died a short while ago at Krook's in Lincoln's Inn. And her mother is... you."

For a moment, Lady Dedlock was stunned into silence.

"Please go," she begged him. When she was alone, she went to her bedroom and wept, thankful that Sir Leicester, in his study, could not hear her tears through the thick walls.

"My child, my child," she sobbed in agony. "Not dead in the first hours of life as my cruel sister told me, but alive. Brought up by my sister, who told me she'd never see me again after my disgrace. Oh Esther, my child."

Lady Dedlock now desperately wished for two things: one, to see her dead love's grave, and two, to embrace her daughter.

Quickly she disguised herself, slipping on a shabby black dress belonging to Hortense, her maid. No one would recognize her, or even see her. It was almost dark; the short winter afternoon was extinguished by clouds of sooty chimney smoke and fog.

She made her way to Lincoln's Inn and Krook's shop. Outside the entrance, a ragged boy swept the frosty street.

"Are you Jo?" she asked him, remembering Mr. Tulkinghorn's words.

"Yep, my lady."

"I'm not a lady. I'm a servant."

"Huh!" said Jo, because he could see her hands were white and soft, not rough with work.

"Tell me, Jo, do you know where Nemo is buried?"

Jo nodded.

"If you show me, I'll give you more money than you've ever had in your life."

Shouldering his broom, Jo led her through an ugly archway to a rusty iron gate, where rats scuttled in the misty swirls of fog. Beyond the gate was a graveyard. The gate was locked.

"They put him there," said Jo. "In the paupers' ground."

She strained her eyes in the darkness, shuddering at the stench. "Is it blessed?" she asked.

Jo stared. "Dunno. Don't make the bones any different if it's blessed or not."

Lady Dedlock wept again, mourning the tragedy of Captain Hawdon's wasted life, and remembering how they had loved each other so many years ago. Then she pulled herself together, gave Jo some money, and walked away. Finding herself outside Mr. Tulkinghorn's house, on an impulse, she rang the bell.

Mr. Tulkinghorn himself answered the door. "What do you want, Lady Dedlock?" he asked. He could not read her eyes. Was it fear or anger that made them flash?

"I've decided to run away," she told him. "My husband will be horrified when he discovers that I, whom he so admires, have brought shame to his name. My disappearance will only be a relief to him. I have left my jewels behind. And you see I wear my servant's dress, so no one will know me."

"If you disappear," Mr. Tulkinghorn replied, "you will make it a hundred times more obvious that you have a wicked secret. I may reveal it. I may not. But you'd be wise to stay put."

"I will do as I think best," she flung at him, storming out. But as soon as she shut the front door, her brave, challenging manner vanished. Her face was twisted in distress, she clasped her hands behind her head, her hair flew wild and undone.

She sped to Mr. Jarndyce's London house, praying that Esther was there.

"Lady Dedlock!" Esther exclaimed, amazed, as she opened the door.

"Come, my child," urged Lady Dedlock. "Never mind the cold and fog; let's go to the garden. I have something secret – but so important – to tell you."

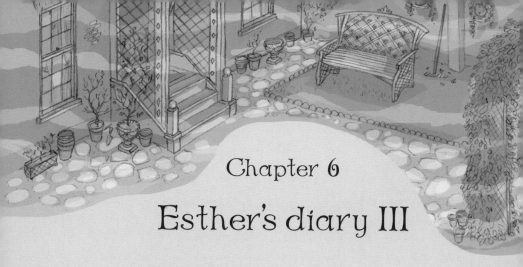

Chapter 6

Esther's diary III

Something has happened while we have been staying with Mr. Jarndyce in London. Something amazing... and shattering. Lady Dedlock came. "I have something to tell you," she said. We went to the garden. She took me in her arms, kissed me, and then she cried, "Oh my child, forgive me! I am your unhappy, wicked mother!"

I begged her to stop crying. I told her I'd always longed to find her. Whatever she'd done, she had my forgiveness; my heart overflowed with love.

"It's too late," she murmured. "I must travel my dark road alone. I am beyond help. I have brought disgrace to those I love."

"No!" I insisted.

"I was told you died at birth," she continued.
"My sister took you and brought you up, hidden
from me. If I had only known! But, darling child,
these kisses must be for the last time. We shall never
meet again. I cannot let my husband suffer for my
wrongs. People are so cruel. They would mock him
and I can't let that happen. It's better if I disappear."

I could not persuade her otherwise. As quickly
as she came, she left. I was shaken. Would it have
been better if I had never been born? If I had not
breathed, would the world have been happier?

I wish I were at Bleak House, not here in London.
Whenever I am unhappy or hurt, I always feel at
peace there, sheltered in its walls. It is truly home.

Chapter 7

Murder

After Lady Dedlock's visit, Mr. Tulkinghorn remained in his study. He wondered about going for a walk, but decided it was too foggy. Thoughtfully, he drew the curtains. If only the window had reflected not the fog but the future and warned him: "Leave the house!" If only the curtains had whispered one word to him: "Go!"

Again the doorbell rang. This time it was Lady Dedlock's maid. She slipped inside, as excited as a wild cat. "I, Hortense, take my revenge on Lady Dedlock," she hissed. "You promised you would reward me for information about her. So I will tell you: she has run away, wearing my clothes. Now pay me."

"But I already know that," said Mr. Tulkinghorn. "I owe you nothing."

"Give me money," she shrieked.

Mr. Tulkinghorn decided that Hortense was no longer useful to him. "If you ever come here again demanding money, I will send for the police," he snapped.

"If you do that," cried Hortense, shaking her fist, "I will prove to them that you are a wicked cheat!"

"Be careful with your threats," Mr. Tulkinghorn began menacingly, and a gun shot rang out.

He slumped in his chair, a red stain spreading from his heart. Hortense flew from the room, swift and silent, like an animal on the run.

Chapter 8

Esther's diary IV

Mr. Guppy has proposed! He sank down on one knee. I said "No," because I don't love him at all. Everything here is sad and mixed-up right now. You know how Mr. Jarndyce has been so good to Richard, paying for his training and giving him a home. Now Richard says he will fight Mr. Jarndyce in court to win the Jarndyce case. Mr. Jarndyce is very upset.

"How could you?" Ada sobbed to Richard.
"I've got big debts," Richard confided.
"Debts?" repeated Ada. "Why?"
Richard smiled. He has such a sunny manner.
"I like living well. What's wrong with having everything I want? I need to win the case to pay my bills. Don't bother your pretty little head about business, Ada."
Oh, Richard! I so wish you weren't like that.

I told Mr. Jarndyce that Mr. Guppy had discovered my parents, but I kept my mother's secret and did not say who she was.

"I'm glad you've learned the truth at last," Mr. Jarndyce said. "Be proud of who you are, Little Woman." He is so wise.

Allan Woodcourt came to visit. While we were talking, the doorbell rang. It was Mr. Bucket, the police inspector. "The lawyer Mr. Tulkinghorn has been murdered," he announced.

"On the night in question, Jo the road sweeper says a lady dressed like a servant spoke to him, before going in to see Mr. Tulkinghorn. And then she visited you. That lady is Lady Dedlock, who has since disappeared. It is a most interesting coincidence."

114

I saw he suspected my mother of murder! It could not be true. "Lady Dedlock was unhappy, not angry," I said. "Let me talk to this Jo," I added. "Maybe he'll tell me more than he told you."

"I'll come too," Allan said.

We went together through the streets to Lincoln's Inn and found Jo, lying on the pavement and shivering with fever.

"Why aren't you at home, in bed?" I asked.

"Ain't got no home!" he muttered, coughing.

It's dreadful that children like Jo are ragged and starving. Something's wrong with the world when the rich are too rich and the poor are so unhappy. "Come with me, Jo," I said. "I'll take care of you."

I took him home and nursed him. He had smallpox. When Jo was slightly better, he told me he had shown my mother Nemo's graveyard – he told me where it was. Then he followed her and saw her enter and leave Mr. Tulkinghorn's house. Later another woman went in, muttering, "I, Hortense, take my revenge," and he heard a shot.

I told Mr. Bucket, and he is going to arrest Hortense, my mother's maid, for murder.

✳✳✳

Catastrophe has hit us. Jo was getting worse, growing more fragile with every hour.

"It's very dark," he said last night, as I sat with him. His eyes were now too weak to see; I could tell his life was fading fast. Stroking his hand, I said, "Our Father, which art in Heaven."

"Our Father," whispered Jo, as softly as a leaf falling from a tree... then he was silent. Poor boy, killed by disease, poverty and neglect. I can't bear it. I can't stop shivering. It must be because I'm so unhappy. My head aches.

***

I haven't written my diary for weeks, because I've been ill. I caught smallpox from Jo. This morning, I asked Ada for a mirror so I could brush my hair.

"No, Esther," she said. "No mirror for you."

"Why?" I asked. She turned away, weeping. But I made her bring one. As soon as I glanced in the glass, I understood.

Smallpox has scarred my face – I think forever.
I am ugly... so ugly... Mr. Jarndyce says there's no
difference really, because I'm still the same person
underneath it all. Wise though he is, I can't believe
him. I'm miserable. Allan will never think me
pretty now.

Ada told me that she and
Richard secretly married
while I was ill. "He's
made lots of wrong
decisions," she said,
"but because I love
him, I'll support him,
rich or poor. He's still
hoping to win the
Jarndyce case."

I couldn't help a
twinge of envy. Ada
has Richard. I'm so
hideous, no one will
ever want me.

Chapter 9

The case is closed

Sir Leicester Dedlock was alone in his house in the country, unable to sleep or eat properly. "If only my wife would come back," he repeated, again and again. "Whatever she's done, I love her. Whatever has happened, I forgive her. I just want her home."

No one could comfort him. No one knew where she was. He asked the police to look for her but they found no clues. She seemed to have vanished without trace.

He stumbled around in despair and frustration. He thought of her all the time, picturing her cold, hungry and lonely, until he turned from his imaginings with a howl of misery to cry once more, "I would forgive you – everything. Come back, come back."

121

Esther remained in London, too ill to return to Bleak House. Gradually, she recovered and her scars began to fade. Allan Woodcourt came to visit her often...

"I don't want his pity," Esther thought. "I wish he wouldn't come. I'm not pretty enough for him. Why can't he stay away?"

"Have you heard the news?" Allan asked on his next visit.

"Tell us," replied Mr. Jarndyce, glad of any diversion to cheer Esther up.

"*Jarndyce and Jarndyce* is over. The case is finished."

"But who has won?" asked Mr. Jarndyce.

"No one," Allan explained. "The money finally ran out. It all disappeared into the lawyers' pockets, because the case had lasted for so many years. There's not a penny left!"

"Poor Richard!" exclaimed Esther.

"Best thing that could have happened to him," comforted Mr. Jarndyce. "Now he knows *Jarndyce* is over, he'll be much steadier. Ada will be happier, too."

"What about you, Mr. Jarndyce?" asked Esther. "It means you'll never be rich either."

"I don't mind," he smiled. "I have enough for my needs. Who needs more?"

"Will you come for a walk, Esther?" Allan asked.

"Oh, no..." she replied quickly, touching her face.

"Go, my dear," urged Mr. Jarndyce. "Your scars are barely noticeable. You're looking so much better."

"We can go where you like..."

Allan smiled, trying to encourage her.

Esther considered. "I'd like to see my father's grave. Jo told me where he's buried," she said.

"We'll go now," promised Allan.

On the way, he asked her to marry him.

"B... but Allan," she stuttered, torn between surprise and delight, "I look so horrible. I thought you could never..."

"The scars don't matter. I've always loved you, anyway."

"But... I am..." The terrible words she had heard in her childhood still haunted her. "I am my mother's disgrace."

"I know the secret," Allan assured her. "Mr. Guppy told Mr. Jarndyce, who told me. I met your mother, and admired her. I love you, Esther, because your heart is soft and your mind is strong, and you are kind to rich and poor alike. So, will you...?"

"Oh yes! I love you too. I always have."

They had reached the entrance to the graveyard, but a crowd had collected at the entrance, blocking the way.

The crowd surrounded a woman who was lying by the gate, one arm hooked through it, as though she embraced it.

"Let me through," cried Allan. "I'm a doctor."

He knelt by the woman's side, and Esther saw a look of compassion on his face. "Come, darling," he said to Esther. "Yours should be the first hands to touch her."

Resolutely Esther crept forward, though she was full of foreboding. She lifted the head, and turned the face. It was her mother, cold and dead. By her side was a note.

This place where I lie down has often been in my mind. Farewell. Forgive.

Chapter 10

Esther's diary, five years later

To anyone who reads my diary, I want it to be known – after sadness and tragedy there is happiness. Joy is stronger than despair.

Allan and I love each other so much. He is a wonderful husband. Mr. Jarndyce has been extraordinarily kind, too. When I told him that Allan had proposed, he said, "Little Woman, if I were younger, I would have married you myself. Allan Woodcourt is a fortunate man. I want to give you a wedding present. I know you love Bleak House. It is yours. I pray you will be blessed with children and that the sun will shine upon your marriage forever."

And all this came true...

"Esther," said Allan this morning, drawing my arm through his. "Do you look in the glass?"

"You know I do," I frowned. "You see me do it."

"Don't you know you are prettier than you ever were?"

"I'm not sure that's true," I laughed. "But I do know that I have two pretty daughters and a handsome husband, and that's quite enough beauty for one house."

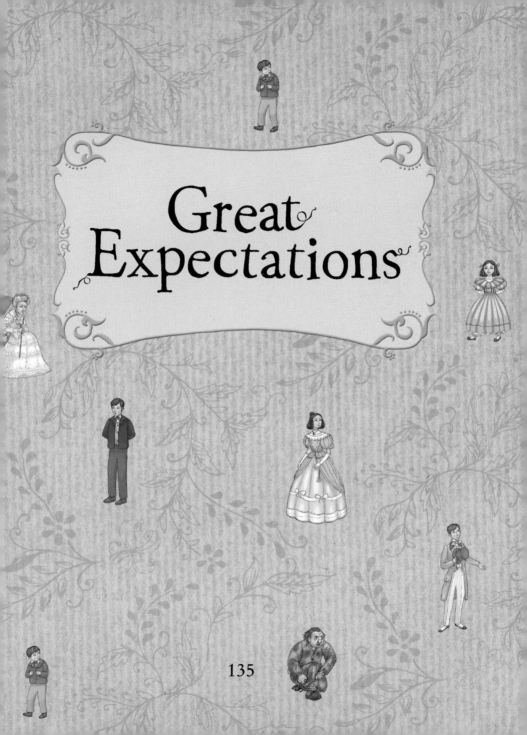

Great Expectations

Contents

Chapter 1

The man in the mist

The churchyard was damp and overgrown. I crouched among the nettles, by the graves of my father, my mother and my little brothers. The wind roared around me and twenty miles away, across the marsh, the sea howled. Mist and fog waved long white fingers through the churchyard. "Death has stolen everyone I loved," I thought, and began to cry.

"Stop that noise, you little devil, or I'll cut your throat!"

A hand suddenly grabbed my shoulder, and, turning, I saw a man burst through the mist into view – a terrible wild-haired man. His clothes were wet, torn and smothered in mud; his shoes were worn through, his teeth chattered. Locked on his legs was a chain that dragged and clanged as he shook me fiercely.

"Don't hurt me! Please!" I begged, in terror.

"What's your name, boy?" he growled.
"Quick!"

"Pip, Sir."

"Where do you live, Pip?" He gripped my wrists.

"Down there, Sir," I nodded. "Past the church. With Joe, the blacksmith, and his wife. That's my sister, Sir."

"Blacksmith, eh?" He pushed me down onto a tombstone, so that his eyes beamed down on mine, and mine looked helplessly up at his.

"You know what a file is, Pip?" he asked.

"Y-Yes, Sir. It's a saw that goes through iron."

"Get me one, first thing in the morning. Get me food, too, or I'll rip out your heart. Don't think you're safe. I know where you live."

"I-I w-w-will," I stammered.

"Swear it. Say Lord strike you dead if you don't."

I said it, and he let go of me. Terrified, I ran home, fast, turning just once to see him jump over the churchyard wall and disappear into the empty black marsh.

My sister met me with a broomstick, which she whacked against my bottom.

"Curse the boy!" she yelled. "Late again. No supper for you!"

As she spoke, a loud BANG! exploded in my ears, like a huge gun.

"What's that?" I cried.

"The police," said my sister, grimly.

"What are they doing?"

"They're firing to warn of an escaped prisoner from the Hulk."

"Please, what's the Hulk?" I asked.

My sister shook me. "Where you'll end up if you don't stop asking questions. It's a prison-ship for bad people, like murderers and robbers." She pushed me with the end of the broomstick. "Go up to bed. Now!"

I didn't starve that night because kind Joe crept up secretly with some supper for me. But my dreams were haunted by an evil villain with clanking chains, and I kept waking, terrified he'd come for me.

At dawn I went down, took Joe's file from his forge – I knew he wouldn't mind once he understood – and stole a big pork pie and a bottle of brandy from the kitchen. My sister, unlike Joe, would be furious when she discovered the theft, and I prayed she wouldn't guess the thief was me.

Chapter 2

The strange bride

The man was waiting for me by the churchyard. "Bless you, boy," he grunted, seizing the stuff from my hands. He gulped the brandy and tore sharp, snapping bites off the pie, like a dog.

Then he grabbed the file and began sawing at his chain, his eyes shifting sideways as if expecting danger from everywhere. "I shan't forget you, boy," he said. "Remember me. Abel Magwitch, that's my name."

"I won't forget you, Sir," I said. I meant it. I knew he'd disturb my thoughts forever. He was still sawing as I ran back home over the marsh.

Inside, I found Joe and my sister with a
visitor, Mr. Jaggers, the lawyer. He looked me
up and down through his bushy eyebrows,
like a judge. I thought my sister had
summoned him because I was a thief and I
shook in my shoes.

"You're lucky, Pip," Joe put in, relieving
my fears.

"You should be grateful," my sister interrupted. "Mr. Jaggers says Miss Havisham wants you to visit her. Today."

I was stunned. Miss Havisham was a rich old woman who lived in a large house in our village and never saw anyone.

My sister washed my face and hair, kneading her hands into my scalp until I saw stars. But no matter how many questions I asked, she couldn't throw light on why Miss Havisham wanted me.

Mr. Jaggers and I arrived at Miss Havisham's gate. Behind was an overgrown courtyard.

Mr. Jaggers, swelling with importance, jangled the bell and a very pretty, haughty-looking girl arrived.

"You must be Pip," she said, looking at me. Then she turned to Mr. Jaggers. "Do you want to see Miss Havisham?" she asked.

"If she wants to see me," Mr. Jaggers replied, expectantly.

"She doesn't," said the girl. Then she pulled me through the gate and closed it, leaving Mr. Jaggers staring after us.

In we went. All the passages were dark. At last we stopped outside a large, oak door.

"Go in," she ordered.

"After you," I said, more in shyness than politeness.

"Don't be ridiculous," she replied, walking away. "I'm not going in."

Half-afraid, I pushed open the door and found myself in a large room, well-lit with wax candles, but without a drop of daylight. Seated in a chair, her elbow on a table, her head resting on her hand, was the strangest lady I had ever seen.

She wore white, like a bride. A long
white veil hung from her head. Even her
hair was white. Then I realized that all the
things I thought were white were faded and
yellow. The flowers in her hair were dead and
withered, and the bride within the dress was
old and withered too.

The dining table, laid for a feast, was hung with cobwebs that draped over the candlesticks. Towering over them, like a black fungus, was an ancient wedding cake. I could see spiders scurrying in and out.

"Look at me," she said, turning her sunken eyes to me. "Are you afraid of a woman who has not seen the sun since before you were born?"

"No," I lied.

"Do you know what I touch here?" she asked, laying one hand upon the other on her left side.

"Your heart, ma'am?" I queried.

"Broken!" she said eagerly, smiling a strange smile that had a kind of boast in it. "I am tired," she went on. "I want to see a child play. So play! Play!"

I couldn't. I didn't know what to do.

"Are you sulking? Are you obstinate?" she demanded.

"N-No," I stammered.

"Call Estella," she ordered.

To shout for the snooty girl was as bad as being told to play. But I did, and she came down the dark corridor with a candle.

"Play," insisted Miss Havisham.

Estella looked horrified. "With this common, clumsy boy?"

"Well," she murmured, "you can break his heart." I couldn't believe my ears. It seemed such a strange and terrible thing to say.

We played cards until Estella won.

"Come here!" ordered Miss Havisham, beckoning me over. "Do you think she's pretty?" she asked in a whisper.

"Yes," I whispered back. "But she's very insulting."

"Hah!" I think she looked pleased. "Go now, Pip. Come again next week."

Estella led me back to the gate. Just as I was leaving, she smiled at me, tilting her face up to mine. "So you think I'm pretty?" she asked.

"Very pretty," I said.

"Am I still insulting?" she asked softly.

"Not as much as when I arrived," I replied.

"No?" she responded, and slapped my face with all the strength she had.

"What do you think of me now, you foul little monster?"

I refused to answer.

Chapter 3

Lucky lad

Back home, my sister and Joe were curious, but I didn't feel like telling them anything.

"You behave properly, and she might leave you her fortune," said my sister.

"Pip doesn't need a fortune; he's got a good home here," Joe smiled. "He'll be a blacksmith, just like me."

I sighed. I didn't want to be a blacksmith, like Joe. I wanted to be rich, so that Estella wouldn't despise me.

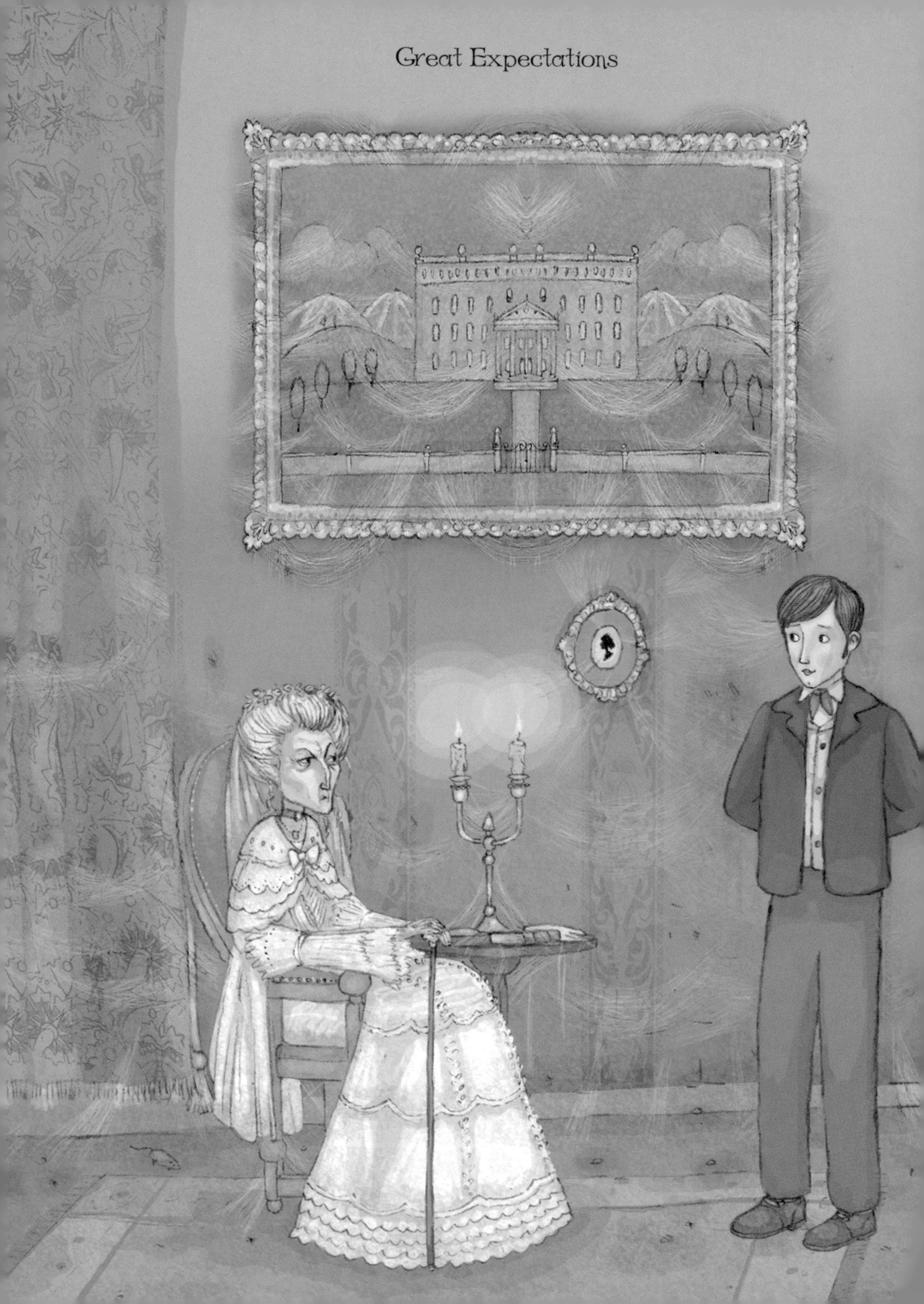

Week after week, year after year, I went to Miss Havisham's house to play with Estella. Nothing ever changed. Wearing her crumbling bride clothes, Miss Havisham stayed indoors, watching over us with her strange smile.

At last the time came when Joe said I was old enough to start work as his apprentice. My dream of being a rich gentleman was at an end. My sister had died suddenly of a fever. I felt I couldn't leave Joe, now he was on his own. I'd have to be a workman, just like him – with thick boots and coarse hands. Estella would never look at me now, I thought. I would be too common for her.

"I won't be able to come any more," I told Miss Havisham on my next visit. "I have to start work."

"Estella is also leaving me," Miss Havisham told me. "She's going to France to finish her education. She must learn to be a grand lady."

Estella was prettier than ever, and still proud, but I felt she wore her pride like a veil, preventing the real Estella from shining through.

I often caught glimpses of her sweetness, even a sadness, that made me wish I could rescue her from her frozen tower.

"I am what Miss Havisham has made me," she confided one day. "I can't help being cold and hard. She never taught me to love. I wish I could."

I had wanted to tell her then that I loved her. My mind formed the words that were on the brink of my lips. Couldn't she feel it… couldn't she love me too? But before I could speak she had said quickly, as if she knew what I was thinking, "It's too late, Pip. I can't change myself now."

She had looked so unhappy that my heart felt wrenched in sympathy.

Now, on hearing Miss Havisham's words, my dream that we might one day be friends and equals had evaporated. Estella would be a grand lady, forever beyond my reach.

"I hope Estella will be very happy," I told Miss Havisham. "And you too."

"Huh!" she said, in disgust.

The next day, the lawyer, Mr. Jaggers, came unexpectedly to our house.

"You are fortunate, Pip," he exclaimed. "You are a man of great expectations!"

"What do you mean?" I gasped.

"I have been asked to tell you," he continued pompously, "that you now have a very large amount of money. Further," – he thrust out a restraining hand to stop my torrent of questions – "the person who has given you the money wants you to leave home, and come to London to learn how to be a gentleman."

He seemed to expand with each piece of news. "Furthermore," he concluded, "the name of this person is to remain a profound secret, until the person chooses to reveal it." Joe and I looked at each other, completely amazed. "It must be Miss Havisham," I thought. "She's given me her fortune."

"If you have the slightest suspicion whom you think it might be, you are to keep your thoughts to yourself," said Mr. Jaggers, as if guessing my mind. "That is one condition of the gift."

"So – so you're going to London, Pip," Joe faltered. "You've been my best friend, and now you're going to be a grand gentleman. I'm very glad for you."

I was so excited I couldn't think about anything else. It never occurred to me that I might miss Joe. And I ignored the thought that Joe, now a lonely widower, might miss me.

"You need proper clothes before you come," advised Mr. Jaggers. "And they should not be the clothes of a working man. Go to the best tailor in town. Here's twenty guineas to begin with. And here's my card. Come to my London house in a week's time."

"Yes, sir," I replied, dreaming already of an elegant carriage and thoroughbred horse to carry me in style to my new life.

164

Chapter 4

An unwelcome visitor

I visited Mr. Trabb, the tailor. "I need a suit of fashionable clothes," I announced. "I can pay with cash."

"Don't hurt me by mentioning money," purred Mr. Trabb, flourishing rolls of fine cloth for my inspection.

I suddenly had a pleasant vision of my future. So this is what it was like to be rich. People would be so eager to please me!

A week later I went to Mr. Jaggers in London.

"Now, Pip," he told me. "You are to live with Mr. Herbert Pocket, a cousin of Miss Havisham. He will show you how to hold your knife and fork properly, how to dance, and how to choose wine. In short, he'll make a gentleman of you. Meanwhile the bank will put money in your account every week."

I listened greedily. I could think of no happier life.

"Ah! Here's my housekeeper with the coffee," he finished.

The housekeeper came in carrying a tray. I stared at her, with a shock of recognition. Surely I knew those eyes, that hair... Yet I couldn't think where I'd seen them before.

That afternoon I met Herbert Pocket, who was just my age. "We'll have such fun, Pip!" he cried. "We'll go to clubs and go racing!"

I could see my life was going to be even better than I'd imagined.

"I'm told you know Miss Havisham?" he commented. "Now there's a story!"

"What do you mean?" I asked.

"You don't know it?" said Herbert, astonished.

I shook my head. "I've always wanted to," I said eagerly.

"She was dressed for her wedding, a sumptuous feast laid on the table," Herbert began. "But as she was setting off to the church, her bridegroom ran away. Her life stopped at the moment of her ruined hopes."

"Poor Miss Havisham!" I said. "No wonder she's so sad. And how did Estella come in to her life?"

"She adopted her. No one knew where she came from. Miss Havisham brought her up to break men's hearts, just as hers was broken."

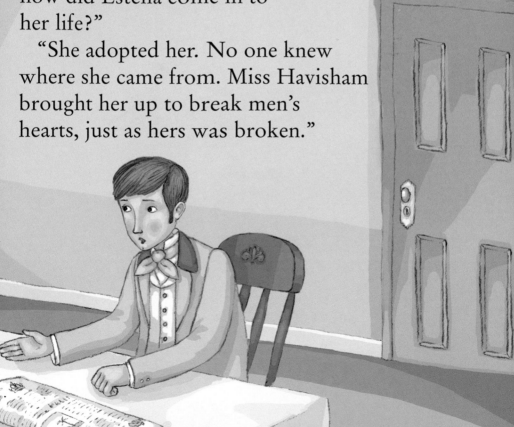

Life with Herbert was packed with amusement. I spent my huge allowance on clothes, good wine and entertainment.

"Why not learn to sail, Pip?" Herbert suggested one day.

I did, and liked it so much that I bought myself a fast boat to race against Herbert's yacht down the Thames.

Before long I was in debt, but I didn't care. Mr. Jaggers always gave me more money when I wanted it.

Joe came to visit me, wearing his shabby country clothes. He fidgeted uncomfortably as my servant let him in.

"You've gone right above me," he said. "London's no place for me. I won't bother you again."

I'm ashamed to say I was glad.

"Miss Havisham wants to see you," he told me, before he left.

I went back to the old house and found Miss Havisham, looking older, and Estella, returned for a while from France, now grown beautiful.

"Love her!" demanded Miss Havisham, playing with Estella's hair. "I adopted her to be loved!"

Silently, I repeated what I'd always known – I love her, I love her. I was amazed that I, once the blacksmith's boy, was destined for her.

"Real love…" mused Miss Havisham. "It's blind, unquestioning. It's humiliating, giving up your whole heart and soul!"

"I know!" I said aloud. "I do love you, Estella. I do!"

"You know that I have no heart," she replied, icy as winter. "I cannot love. I don't even love you, Miss Havisham."

Miss Havisham turned to me then. "What have I done?" she asked. "She's so hard… so cruel."

Estella was so cold and distant, I returned to my London apartment that evening filled with unhappiness. The night was wild and stormy and I came home as fast as I could. On my doorstep a strange man, old and tough-looking, was waiting for me.

"Who are you?" I asked, suspiciously.

"My, you've grown into a fine young gentleman," said the stranger. "Just what I hoped!"

"Y-you'd better come in," I stammered. Because I knew the man! Even though I couldn't recognize his features, I knew him, as though the wind and rain had blown away the years, and had swept us back to the churchyard where we had first met. It was Magwitch, the escaped prisoner.

174

Chapter 5

Secrets

Inside, to my horror, he hugged me.

"You acted nobly, Pip. I never forgot."

"Don't!" I said. "It was nothing. I hope you are no longer a criminal. And now you must understand... Our ways are different... I can't ask you to stay–"

"Wait!" Magwitch ordered. "Didn't you guess where your money came from?"

"What?" I was astonished.

"I got away," Magwitch explained. "I went to Australia, and made a lot of money. I made it for you, Pip. Every penny I saved, I thought, this will help Pip, this will make a gentleman of him."

I was horrified. My money hadn't come from Miss Havisham after all, but from a man who had once been a criminal. It was tainted, dirty money!

"It was hard to come back, Pip," Magwitch continued. "I'm safe in Australia, but here my sentence still stands. If the police find me, I'll be hanged. But I wanted to see you. I wanted to see how my Pip had grown up."

I licked my lips nervously. "Why did you send me your money?"

A look of misery swept over his face. "I had a child once. A little girl. I lost her.

When I saw you on the marsh, you reminded me of her. She was the same age as you then."

"She died?" I queried.

"Who knows?" Magwitch wiped away tears. "I left her with her mother. Then I heard her mother was on trial for murder. God knows what happened to my little girl."

I couldn't help feeling disgusted. Magwitch and his family seemed like filthy rats from the gutter, without morality or decency.

"Don't sneer," Magwitch said. "Growing up isn't easy for poor folk. I've been in and out of jail all my life. I began as a child – begging, lying, thieving…"

He trailed off and looked at me pleadingly, wanting me to understand.

"You can stay here tonight," I muttered.

But I slept badly. Magwitch wasn't safe in England, and I didn't like him being here either.

Leaving him in my apartment the next morning, I went to see Mr. Jaggers.

"I know now where my money comes from," I told him.

"How?" he asked.

"Magwitch is here! He came to see me. And I want to know more."

Mr. Jaggers called his housekeeper to bring us coffee. As she came in, I was struck again by her likeness to someone I knew. This time I realized who it was. The way she held herself, her beauty, though faded now, was unmistakable. My jaw dropped open in amazement. This, surely, was Estella's mother!

Mr. Jaggers watched my face.

"You've guessed right," he said, when she'd left the room. "She is indeed Estella's mother. I was her lawyer when she was arrested for murder, and she was desperate about her daughter. I got her acquitted, but I took the child, and gave her to Miss Havisham, who wanted to adopt a little girl."

"Was it right to take the child from her mother?" I wondered, aloud.

Mr. Jaggers nodded with certainty. "I told her mother: 'If I get you off, I will save your child too.' Consider this, Pip. Estella's father was a criminal. I've seen pauper children of criminals grow up to meet the hangman themselves. Here was one pretty child out of the heap who could be saved."

"I understand. And her father? What happened to him? Who was he?"

Mr. Jaggers poured himself another drink. "Abel Magwitch," he said.

Chapter 6

Stormy seas and quiet waters

I was stunned.

"You must get him out of England as soon as you can," Mr. Jaggers went on. "He has plenty of enemies. If any of them knows he's here, they'll tell the police, and he'll end up dangling from a hangman's rope."

"I'll take him down the river as soon as the tide is right," I said. "Then I'll find a ship to take him to sea."

"One thing, Pip. Estella knows nothing about her parents. Nor does Miss Havisham. Promise you'll never tell."

I swore myself to secrecy. I'd do anything to protect my beautiful Estella.

The following fine night, Magwitch and I rowed down the Thames, past London Bridge, past the barges and oyster boats, until we reached the open sea.

Magwitch had agreed, for my sake, to leave the country. Now he sat back smiling, smoking his pipe. "You know, Pip, dear boy," he said, "I'm happy. You've turned out well, and I'm still free."

He spoke too soon. Another vessel drew alongside in the dark, and a policeman leaped out into our boat.

"Abel Magwitch, I arrest you in the name of the law," he announced.

But Magwitch would not be taken so easily. As the policeman handcuffed him he fought back, then threw himself into the sea.

His eyes grew frantic with fright as he tried desperately to swim. He couldn't do it; his hands were chained behind his back. In an instant I jumped in after him. I had to save him! As I heaved his cold body inside the boat, the policeman looked down at us.

"If he ain't dead after tonight's activities, he'll get what he deserves when he comes before the judge!" he observed.

"He must go to a hospital," I said firmly, and to my relief, this was allowed.

Magwitch was very ill. His time in the icy water, being half-drowned, was too much for his old heart. I stayed by his side every day. I realized how kind and true he'd been to me all these years. I wanted to do all I could in return.

"You've stuck by me, even though I'm under a dark cloud," he wheezed, coughing. His breath was very uneven. "I'm proud of you, Pip."

His voice grew fainter. "Dear boy," he managed to say. Then… silence.

I held his hand in mine. "You had a child once, whom you loved and lost. Can you understand what I say?"

He answered with a faint squeeze of my hand.

"She is alive and has good friends. She is a beautiful lady, and I love her."

With a last movement he raised my hand to his lips. Then a quiet look came into his eyes and his head rolled gently to one side.

Chapter 7

The heart of the fire

"You won't get Magwitch's money, now he's dead," Mr. Jaggers told me the next day. "Since he was an escaped criminal and died in England, the State owns everything he had."

I thought quickly. I had lived extravagantly and had large debts. I would have to earn my own way now. "I'll be a blacksmith after all," I announced. "I'm sure Joe will have me back."

Joe was as kind and generous as he'd always been. "It'll be like old times, you and me together, Pip," he smiled. "Just what I always wanted."

He never mentioned the time he'd come to London, when I hadn't been very welcoming. I saw now that Joe was the true gentleman, while I'd turned into a snob. I hated myself.

"Thank you, Joe," I said. "I'll never have a better friend than you."

I said goodbye to my friends in London, promising Herbert that I would write to him.

"Why don't you visit Miss Havisham again?" Joe asked. "It would be a friendly thing to do."

I thought he was right. I ought to.

She wept when I saw her, and sank on her knees. To see her thus, her white hair and worn face at my feet, shocked me.

"It's Estella!" she sobbed. "I've wronged her! I wanted to save her from a fate like mine. I stole her heart and put ice in its place."

I knew that was true. She'd taken a happy little girl and made her into a copy of her own despair. I saw too that in shutting herself up, living in the past, she'd cut herself off from the healing influences of normal life. Her whole mind had grown diseased.

"Oh Pip!" she wept. "What have I done?"

I tried to comfort her.

190

Finally I left her, giving a last glance at the room. I had a strange feeling I'd never return.

In that second I saw a candle tumble from its candlestick and fall onto Miss Havisham's dress. Instantly, faster than my dash to extinguish it, a great flame leaped up as she ran at me, shrieking. A whirl of fire blazed all around her and soared to the ceiling, lighting the crumbling wedding feast, the cobwebs and candelabra, in an intense red and orange light.

I took her in my arms and swept her outside, watching in horror as flames licked my arms, too. Scraps of tinder, that a moment ago had been her faded bridal dress, floated in the smoky air and fell in a black shower. I carried her into the garden and wrapped her in my coat to smother the flames, all the while calling for help.

I tried to ignore the searing pain where the flames had caught me, too. And behind me, the fire devoured the house.

At last, a doctor came. She began to speak as he tended to her, and I bent over her to catch her low and wandering voice.

"When the child first came, I meant to save her from misery like mine."

And then:

"Forgive me..."

After that, the world around me turned dark, and I felt and heard nothing.

I woke some weeks later, in my old bed at Joe's house.

"You've been very ill, Pip," Joe said, spooning medicine into my mouth. "You were badly burned in that fire."

"Miss Havisham?" I asked. "How is she?"

"I'm afraid she's dead, Pip," he replied gently.

As soon as I felt stronger, I walked to the ruins of Miss Havisham's house. A cold silvery mist hid the blackened stones. As I came nearer, I saw a woman approach me.

"Estella!" I cried.

She seemed tired, her face pale and drawn, with a look I had never seen before... a saddened, softened light in those once proud eyes.

"I came back from France as soon as I heard of her death," she said. "Poor Miss Havisham! I thought of you often, Pip. You were kind to her."

"I was fond of her. She was unhappy," I replied.

"I'm going to sell the land," she went on. "It will be built on. Something else will take the place of that sad house..."

"Estella..." I interrupted.

She looked up at me. She seemed unsure of herself. "Tell me we are friends," she whispered.

"We will always be friends. I've always loved you," I said, reaching out for her.

Hand in hand, we walked out of the ruins. The mist was rising. I saw no shadows before us, only the clear air, calm and still. I knew Estella and I would never be parted again.

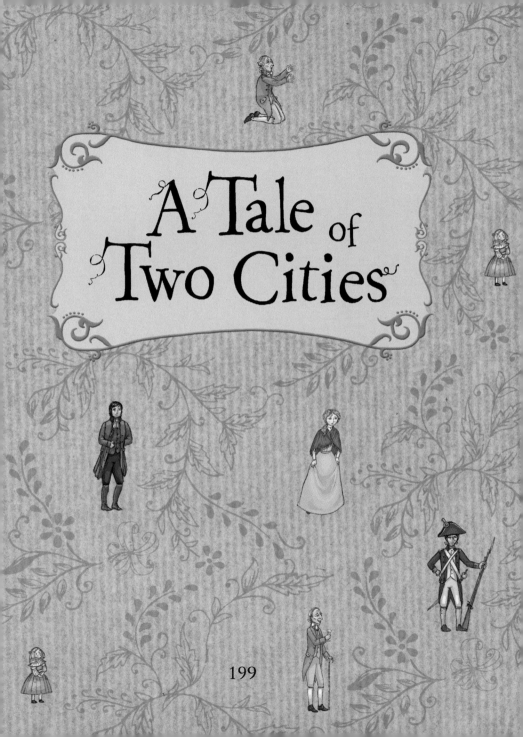

A Tale of Two Cities

Contents

Chapter 1

Paris 1775

"Out of my way, peasants!" The Marquis d'Evrémonde stuck his head out of his golden carriage as it thundered over the cobbles.

"My baby," shrieked a woman, snatching up her toddler from under the murdering, careless wheels.

"What's one brat more or less?" drawled the Marquis, tossing the woman a coin. "Now you have fewer mouths to feed. I hope it hasn't injured my horses."

As he swept past, the woman broke down, weeping bitterly over the still, little body.

"Another Evrémonde crime," Madame Defarge announced, knitting busily. She sat on a chair outside her wine shop, watched by a man unloading wine casks. Click! Click! Click! went her needles.

"What are you knitting?" he asked.

With a sinister smile, Madame Defarge stroked her work lovingly. "Names," she said, stretching it out. "See – Evrémonde's name is already knitted in. This way, we know who we will punish… one day… when we are ready…"

As the man looked, a wine cask slipped from his arms, smashing into fragments. A red river of wine flowed down the street.

Instantly, all the people within reach rushed
to drink it up. They were wild-looking,
ragged and gaunt with hunger. With screams
of pleasure, some knelt to scoop their hands
in it; some sucked the splintered wood; others
dipped rags in it and squeezed the drops down
their throats.

One man, laughing crazily, plunged his finger
in the dirty crimson liquid and scrawled on a
wall the word: BLOOD.

The day was to come when that too would be spilled on the streets, and the stain of it would lie red upon the stones... because it was the best of times and the worst of times. The rich feasted in palaces while the poor scrabbled like rats for food in the gutter. And while the poor suffered, they dreamed of revolution, to stop the happy, easy life of the rich, who smiled and danced and dreamed of parties.

Chapter 2

The living ghost

"This is the place," whispered Lucie Manette, her eyes alight with excitement and a little fear. She stepped through the puddles of wine, past Madame Defarge, into the shop.

"Excuse me," she said hesitantly to the man behind the counter. "I've heard that my father, Dr. Manette, is here."

"So he is," said Monsieur Defarge. "Come with me."

"Then it's true," gasped Lucie. "He's alive?"

"Only just. He's been imprisoned in the Bastille for eighteen years. When he was set free, we brought him here for safety... and to plan our revenge."

"Careful what you say," warned Madame Defarge. "The girl's a stranger..."

"A long time ago, I was your father's servant," Monsieur Defarge continued. "He was a good man, a doctor. Everybody loved your father."

A strange emptiness swept over Lucie as she tried to imagine what eighteen years of captivity would do to a man. "*Was* a good man? Is he... not well?"

Monsieur Defarge was silent, and took Lucie up the stairs. At the top, he unlocked the attic door.

"You lock him in?" Lucie was appalled.

"He knows nothing else. He'd be terrified
– rave – tear himself to pieces if the door was
left open."

"That's awful," she thought, shuddering with
dread. "Awful... I must be brave."

As she entered the attic she saw a white-haired
man with a hollow face, sitting on a bench in the
window. He was stooped forward, completely
engrossed, making shoes.

"Hard at work, I see," said Monsieur Defarge, gently.

After a long pause the head was lifted. "Yes."

The voice was faint, like a feeble echo of a sound made long ago. The eyes looked up, not with any interest, but with a dull, mechanical glance, then returned to gaze at the shoe in his hand.

"Where did you learn to make shoes?" asked Monsieur Defarge.

"Here... in prison... I asked leave to..." said the faraway voice.

"I have a visitor for you. Can you tell her your name?"

A weary sigh. "One Hundred and Five, North Tower."

"He doesn't know his name?" said Lucie.

The man seized his knife, pointing it at Lucie, gasping, "What... who... is this?"

Monsieur Defarge leapt forward to protect her, but she was not afraid.

She folded her father's hands in hers, and kissed them.

Wonderingly, he touched her long golden hair. "My wife had hair like this! Are you an angel?"

Lucie burst into tears. "I am your daughter!" she sobbed, hugging him. "My mother is dead, but you – oh! You shall be restored to life, I promise. Come back with me to England, to be at peace."

He collapsed on the floor. Lucie knelt too, cradling his head, her hair shielding him like a soft curtain. "Please," she implored Monsieur Defarge, "Get us away from Paris now, this instant."

"I'm not sure he's well enough."

"Better to risk the journey than to stay one more hour in this terrible city where he has suffered so much."

"Well, I wish you luck, Lucie Manette." Monsieur Defarge helped the old man to stand. "Are you glad to be restored to life?" he asked.

Back came the answer in that faraway, sunken voice. "I don't know."

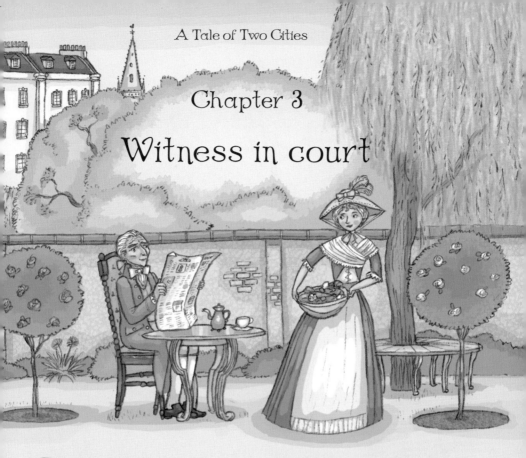

Chapter 3

Witness in court

The journey back to England was hard, but Lucie and her father were helped by a fellow passenger, a man named Charles Darnay. Five years later, Dr. Manette was a different man, strong and healthy, and working as a doctor again. He and Lucie lived in a nice little house in London with a quiet, pretty garden.

"Please God," Lucie prayed daily, "let the bad times be forgotten forever." But then, one day, a summons came through the door.

Dr. Manette and Lucie Manette must attend the Royal Courts of Justice as witnesses in a trial for treason.

They had no choice but to obey. The man on trial was Charles Darnay. Now they learned that he was suspected of being a spy...

"Answer truthfully," a lawyer told Lucie. "Have you seen this man before?"

Lucie stared at the prisoner with pity and admiration. She hesitated, painfully aware the punishment for spying was hanging. "Yes," came her whisper.

"Go on," ordered the lawyer.

"We met him on the boat from France. He was so kind... My father was very ill, and he helped me look after him."

"Did he have papers with him?"

"Yes, I think so..."

"Hmm..." The lawyer paused.

Suddenly, another lawyer stood up. "Look at the prisoner, my Lord, and look at me. Are we not like twins? No one could say for certain that Mr. Darnay was not myself, Sydney Carton, or that Sydney Carton was not Mr. Charles Darnay! No one could be sure, therefore, that it was Mr. Darnay on the boat. Perhaps I ought to be charged with treason too."

Everyone in court laughed. The two men did look extraordinarily like each other, though Sydney Carton was untidy and slouching, while Charles Darnay was upright and much cleaner.

The judge thumped his fist on his desk. "Case dismissed. The prisoner is acquitted."

Afterwards, Sydney Carton came across Charles in the corridor.

"Thank you – with all my heart!" Charles exclaimed. "You helped a complete stranger."

"It was nothing," laughed Sydney. "Tell me – are you a spy? You're French..."

"Half French; my mother was English. Of course I'm not a spy. I'm a French teacher, and loyal to Britain."

"So how does it feel," asked Sydney, lowering his voice, "when a golden-haired doll like Miss Lucie Manette can't take her eyes off you?"

Charles flushed. "How dare you..." he began.

"Don't be offended." Sydney slapped him on the back. "And don't be so moral! I'm a bit drunk. I usually am. Life's too dull, otherwise."

He strolled off, looking back as people pressed up to Charles, congratulating him on his narrow escape from death.

Now Lucie was shaking Charles's hand, blushing as she smiled up at him.

"I bet they're arranging to meet again," Sydney muttered, watching them. "He's everything I'm not... more handsome... easy, pleasing manners. If only I were him, a pretty pair of blue eyes would be smiling on me. Huh!"

For comfort he went to a pub, drank a pint of wine, and fell fast asleep. The candles burned down, dripping wax onto his hair as it straggled all over the table, but Sydney Carton, the brilliant lawyer whose laziness had ruined every chance life had offered, didn't know and didn't care.

Chapter 4

The quiet before the storm

The Manettes asked Charles Darnay to visit them. Lucie suggested they ask Sydney too. It was the first of many tea parties, under the weeping willow in the Manettes' peaceful London garden. Sydney began to admire Lucie, not just for her beauty, but for her sweetness and strength of character.

It was obvious, though, that she loved Charles. Sydney grew increasingly moody and hated himself for it, but his feelings for Lucie and his jealousy of Charles made it hard for him to stop.

"I'd do anything for you," he told her one day.

"Please don't say that," she begged, not wanting to hurt him.

"Charles is a fine man, better than I could ever be."

"Couldn't you... try to drink less, work harder...?"

She was surprised to see tears in his eyes. Never had she seen him so softened. It gave her confidence to go on. "I believe in you, Sydney. I wish I could help you..."

"You have... you inspire me. You make me think about starting again... but it's all a dream. I'm like one who has died young – wasted, drunk... I'm glad you don't love me; I'd drag you down with me."

Lucie, desperately sad for him, tried to find words to comfort him. Sydney interrupted her silence. "I know you will marry Charles. Remember this, though. I'd give my life to make you happy. Keep this conversation secret. God bless you."

Soon after, Lucie accepted Charles Darnay's proposal of marriage.

"Now I must ask your father's permission," Charles said.

He found Dr. Manette working in the garden. "I know how much Lucie loves you," he told the Doctor, "and I never want to come between you." He spoke of his desire to marry Lucie and started to explain his background. "You know I'm half French..."

"Stop!" shuddered Dr. Manette. "I don't want to hear about France, ever again."

"I must tell you. Darnay isn't my real name; it's my mother's. My real name is Evrémonde. My uncle is the Marquis, and I am his heir. But I hate his cruelty, and that's why I've made a new life for myself in England."

"Oh God in Heaven... not that name..."
Evrémonde. It jerked Dr. Manette's memory,
recalling everything he wanted to forget.
Time swung back, and he was once again
inside One Hundred and Five, North Tower,
that cell where he had been buried alive for
so many years and all hope of freedom and
happiness had vanished in the darkness. It was
an Evrémonde who had put him there. Now
Lucie would marry another Evrémonde.

He stumbled into the house, fighting
for breath, struggling with the pain of
remembering. Then, overcome by the
nightmare of prison, his mind went blank.

"Father... where are you?"
Silence.
Lucie had searched everywhere without success. Finally, up in the attic she heard a faint tap, tap. And again, tap, tap, tap. She rushed upstairs and opened the door. There was her father, silhouetted against the window, bent over his tools. He was making shoes.

Chapter 5

The storm breaks

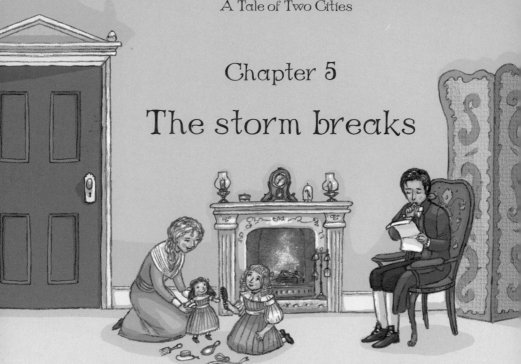

Bravely, Dr. Manette recovered a second time from his madness. Lucie and Charles married, and had a little girl, also named Lucie, as golden-haired as her mother.

They were happy days in that London house, until a letter came for Charles from France. Reading it, his face grew white as ashes.

"What is it, dearest?" asked Lucie.

"I must go to Paris at once."

"Please – no!" said Lucie. "We hear of such terrible things in France now. There will be a revolution, everyone says. You won't be safe."

"I must," Charles repeated. "This letter is about an old servant who was good to me. He's been thrown in prison just because he was employed by my uncle. The letter says my uncle is dead. I'm the Marquis now and it's my duty to help this poor man."

"Darling, DON'T go!" Lucie pleaded, throwing her arms around him. "I'm afraid for you."

"Shhh. You know I must do what's right." He was adamant. He kissed his wife and little Lucie, shook Dr. Manette's hand, and went away.

Days, weeks, then months passed, but not a word did they hear from him. Lucie could bear the silence no longer. "If only we were in Paris," she thought, "I'm sure we would find out what's happened to him." She asked Sydney Carton to accompany herself, her fragile old father and her little girl.

"I'll come," said Sydney at once. "Though it'll be dangerous. There are riots everywhere. Paris is becoming a blood bath."

Lucie hugged little Lucie. "No one will hurt us. Everyone knows the story of Dr. Manette, unjustly imprisoned for eighteen years."

She was right... and terribly wrong.

France was in the grip of a revolution. The poor had become a mighty army, seizing power from the rich. The King was tried, found guilty, and beheaded. So were his wife, their children and a thousand rich aristocrats.

The sharp blade of the Guillotine chopped off so many heads that the ground beneath it was soon rotten red, as red as the wine that had once stained the street outside the Defarges' wine shop.

All this time, Madame Defarge had been knitting steadily, knitting the names of everyone to be exterminated. Click! Click! Click! The stitches slipped off her needles as regularly as the Guillotine chopped off heads. Her mouth stretched in a grim line of satisfaction.

"One big fish we still have to catch," she told her husband, "is young Evrémonde, known as Charles Darnay."

"You want him killed too? I hear he has married good Dr. Manette's daughter."

"Every member of that family must die. Now Darnay's uncle, the wicked Marquis, is dead, he'll return to France... and the Guillotine is hungry for him."

"All right, my love," promised Monsieur Defarge. "We just need to find some evidence against him, and I think I know where to look."

"Where?"

Monsieur Defarge smiled. "Today we storm the Bastille!"

The Bastille! With a roar that sounded as though all the winds of France whistled in that hated word, an army of angry peasants surged to the prison.

Hunger and revenge were their spur; cannon and musket their weapons. Raging fire and smoke blackened the eight great towers and massive stone walls. Wounded soldiers fell into an angry sea of flashing swords, until Defarge and his men swept the drawbridge down.

"Free the prisoners!"

"Unlock the secret cells!"

"Destroy the instruments of torture!"

In the mass of escaping men, Defarge grabbed a prison guard. "Show me One Hundred and Five, North Tower, or I'll cut your throat!"

The terrified guard led him past gloomy cells where daylight had never shone, through hideous doors and dark cages, and up staircases more like dried, crumbling waterfalls than steps.

At last they stopped in a room with four blackened walls, a rusted iron ring in one of them, no window, a worm-eaten stool and a straw bed.

"Pass your torch along these walls," Defarge ordered. In the flickering light he saw initials scratched into the filthy bricks. "A. M.," he read. "That's Alexandre Manette. Yes, this was his cell. Hold your torch higher."

A brick in the chimney looked loose. Grabbing a crowbar from the guard, Defarge smashed at it until it gave way. He fumbled in the dusty crevice behind it and drew out an ancient bundle of papers, which he stuffed in his pocket.

"Say your prayers, Darnay," he laughed triumphantly. "These papers may well be your death sentence."

Chapter 6

The trial

Some weeks later, Lucie, her father, little Lucie and Sydney arrived in Paris. Dodging the riots, they went straight to the Defarge wine shop.

"I'm sure they'll help us," Lucie comforted herself. "They were so good to my father."

"Do you know where my husband is?" she asked Madame Defarge.

"I do," said Madame, checking her knitting. "He's in prison, awaiting trial."

"Why?" asked Sydney. "He's done nothing wrong. He only came to France to help an old servant..."

"He's an aristocrat and an Evrémonde. Of course he is guilty. He must die."

"Help me, please," pleaded Lucie. "You are a woman, like me. You know what love means..."

Coldly Madame Defarge stared at her.

"Oh," cried Lucie, drawing her child to her. "I couldn't bear my Lucie to be fatherless. Have pity, I beg you..."

"So this is Evrémonde's child?" Madame Defarge asked, her needles clicking fast. "Her name is in my knitting."

"What does she mean?" asked little Lucie.

"I don't know," whispered Lucie, a chill in her heart.

"As for your suffering," Madame continued, "why shouldn't you suffer? Do you think other wives and mothers have not suffered? All our lives we have seen poverty, nakedness, sickness, hunger, thirst, misery. Why should you be special? Why should we care about you?"

She left the room, leaving Lucie trembling.

"Don't worry," comforted Sydney. "They can't stop us from going to Charles's trial. We'll soon have him free, I'm sure."

"Once the court knows he's my son-in-law, they won't touch him," added Dr. Manette.

They were forbidden to see Charles until his trial. When they arrived in the courtroom, it was already full of onlookers, jostling for seats like an audience at a play. Monsieur and Madame Defarge sat in the front row.

"Charles Evrémonde, called Darnay, step forward," ordered the judge. "I accuse you of being an aristocrat from an evil family who oppressed the poor."

"Cut off his head," roared the crowd.

"But I live in England now," Charles protested. "With my wife, Lucie Manette, only daughter of Dr. Manette, who sits..." he pointed, "...over there."

This answer pleased the crowd. "Dr. Manette," they whispered, "that brave man..." and some had tears in their eyes.

Dr. Manette felt a leap of hope. "If the court remembers me, we have a chance," he thought. Leaning on his walking stick, he stood up.

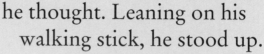

"Set this man free. He is my son-in-law, a good man, a husband and a father. He does not deserve to die."

"Too late. Charles Darnay is condemned," the judge interrupted.

"By whom?" asked Dr. Manette.

"By Monsieur Defarge, wine seller, by Madame Defarge, his wife, and by one other. Alexandre Manette."

Dr. Manette was stunned into silence.

"Tell the court what you did the day the Bastille was stormed, Monsieur Defarge," directed the judge.

Defarge spoke steadily. "I knew Alexandre Manette was imprisoned in One Hundred and Five, North Tower. I went there. I discovered this letter" – he held up a dusty bundle – "in a hole in the wall. It was written by Dr. Manette."

"Read it to the court," said the judge.

Defarge raised his voice so that all could hear the terrible words.

Chapter 7

The letter

I, Alexandre Manette, a doctor, have now been in prison for ten years. All hope of freedom is lost. I write with difficulty; my ink is made of scrapings of soot mixed with my blood.

One day a hand may find this letter's hiding place, when I and my sorrows are dust, to learn how I came to this vile and horrible dungeon...

I was strolling in Paris one moonlit night, when a carriage stopped by me. Inside it was a gentleman disguised in a cloak.

"Are you Dr. Manette?" he asked.

"I am."

"Jump into the carriage. I know a patient who needs your care."

I climbed in. We journeyed far, until we reached a deserted house. I heard piteous cries from upstairs, and found a beautiful girl lying tied to a bed, tossing with fever. She was very ill, and after I untied her, I soothed her with medicine from my bag.

Then I heard groans from above. I rushed upstairs into a loft where I saw a handsome peasant boy on some hay on the ground, bleeding. "He's dying!" I said aloud. I turned around to see the gentleman framed in the doorway. "How did this happen?" I demanded.

"A crazy, common dog! He forced me to draw

my sword on him."

Not a word of pity in this answer.

The boy's eyes opened and fixed on me. "These nobles are very proud," he rasped, "but us common dogs are proud too. Have you seen her – my sister?"

I nodded.

"We are tenants of this... Marquis," he sneered at the word. "We worked for him without pay while he took our crops, our animals, our hens..."

I was amazed that he summoned the strength to speak. And the Marquis just stood by, unmoved.

"When my sister married," the boy continued, "the Marquis admired her and asked her husband to lend her to him. When he refused, the Marquis harnessed him to his carriage like a horse and whipped him 'til he fell down dead."

The Marquis shrugged. "These people are animals. They don't have feelings."

The boy's words kept on flowing. "Then he dragged my sister away. I followed them... I hit him, and he struck me with his sword."

With a massive effort the boy sat up and, gasping, raised his right hand. "Marquis," he panted, "I mark you with my blood, as a sign that you and your accursed family must bear responsibility for your wickedness."

With that he fell back, and stopped breathing. I went upstairs to the girl and stayed with her all night, but there was nothing more I could do for her, and when the cold sun's rays shone upon her at daybreak, she too was dead.

The Marquis said not one word to me. We got into the carriage. I expected it to take me home, but instead it brought me here, to this prison, to my living grave. I could not escape.

I believe in the mark of that boy's blood. I believe that the Marquis d'Evrémonde and all his descendants do not deserve God's mercies. I, Alexandre Manette, declare their wickedness to Heaven and to Earth.

A terrible sound arose, like the baying of wild dogs in the night. A sound of eagerness that meant blood.

"Save him now, Dr. Manette!" cackled Madame Defarge, in triumph. "Save him now. That dead boy was my brother, that dead girl was my sister. Since Evrémonde killed my family, I have sworn to kill every member of the Evrémonde family. Wind and fire may blow and burn themselves out, but nothing shall stop me!"

At every juryman's vote there was a roar. And another and another. "Guilty!" they cried. Roar after roar. It was unanimous. Charles Darnay was condemned to death.

Chapter 8

A life for love

Lucie screamed. She rushed over to him, and he, leaning over the dock, hugged her. "Goodbye, my love. One day we shall meet again – in Heaven," he murmured.

"It won't be long. I feel my heart will break. Don't suffer for me, Charles. I will bear everything, while I live."

"Kiss our child for me."

Dr. Manette had followed her and fell on his knees with a cry of anguish.

"No!" cried Charles. "What have you done that you should kneel to us? I understand now the struggle you went through when you learned my real name. Forgive me. There could never be a happy ending for me."

As he was taken away to prison, little Lucie clung to Sydney Carton.

"Oh Sydney," she sobbed. "Can't you think of something to save Daddy? Look at my mother. I can't bear to see her crying like that. Help me... help me..."

She heard him whisper, "A life for love," before he kissed her gently, put her down and followed Charles. That was what she always remembered, years later, when she was an old lady, telling the story to her grandchildren.

Charles, alone in his cell, paced up and down.

He knew there was no hope for him.

The door opened.

"Sydney!" Charles cried, amazed. "How did you get in here? You're not... surely... a prisoner... like me?"

"Certainly not," Sydney said briskly. "I bribed my way in. Now, listen, Charles. You must do exactly what I say. Take off your boots and put on mine."

"This is madness, Sydney. What are you planning? We can't escape from here. You will only die with me."

"I come from your wife and child, Charles. I repeat, do what I say. Now change your coat for mine. Is your hand steady?"

Charles was shaking, but he said, "I think so..."

"Good. Here are pen and ink. Write what I dictate and take it to Lucie. If the wrong people find it, they must think it's a note from you before you died."

Puzzled, Charles obeyed. He dipped his pen in the ink, and wrote Sydney's words.

Remember our conversation long ago. I give my life to make you happy.

"Now put the paper in your pocket, Charles," ordered Sydney.

"What are you doing?" Charles demanded.

Sydney had crushed a capsule in his hand. He thrust it under Charles's nose.

"Whass... that...?" Charles muttered thickly as he breathed in the fumes. He collapsed on the floor, knocked unconscious by Sydney's powerful drug.

"It's worked," Sydney said aloud. He finished changing into Charles's clothes, then opened the door and summoned the guard he had bribed.

"Carry this man out, put him in a carriage, and send him to Dr. Manette, at this address. Now leave me here, in this cell. Lock me in. Hurry..."

The guard did as he was told. The door closed and Sydney was left alone, but not for long. Soon a jailer came in, rubbing his hands with glee, to send the prisoner on his last journey.

Crowds lined the streets, cheering the Guillotine; cheering Liberty, Equality, Fraternity – and Death. As Sydney walked with other prisoners, a girl pushed through to his side.

"Can I walk with you, Evrémonde?" she faltered. "I'm so scared. They're executing me for conspiracy, but I've done nothing. I'm only a dressmaker."

"Of course you can walk with me," he smiled, looking down at her. She was very young, and she was shivering.

"Oh," she whispered, shocked, as, returning his gaze, she saw him properly. "You're not Evrémonde!" Then, after a pause, "Are you dying for him?"

"And for his wife and child."

Now she was trembling violently. "May I hold your hand? You're so brave."

Sydney put his arm around her. "You will be brave too," he promised.

"Down, Evrémonde!" yelled the crowd as they walked on. "To the Guillotine, all aristocrats!"

"Is the moment nearly here?" asked the young girl. "Will it hurt?"

"No," Sydney assured her. "It's very quick."

"I feel better with you," she murmured.

Sydney kissed her. "Keep your eyes on me until the end. In the world to come, there is no trouble and no unhappiness. Remember that. Bless you."

Courageously, the young girl met her fate, and then it was Sydney's turn.

They said of him that night that his face was the most peaceful the city had ever seen. He looked like a prophet, shining with wisdom, gladdened by his glimpse of the future. And these were the words he whispered to himself...

I see the lives for which I give my life, safe in my beloved England. I know I shall hold a place in their hearts, and in the hearts of their children. I see my Lucie, an old woman, weeping for me on the anniversary of this day. I see her with a child who will be called by my name. I see this child making a success of his life, not, as I did, ruining every chance I had. I know Lucie will tell this child my story, in her loving, tender voice.

It is a far, far better thing that I do, than I have ever done. It is a far, far better rest that I go to than I have ever known.

David Copperfield

Contents

Chapter 1

I am born

My story begins before I was born. It was a bright, windy, March afternoon and my mother, Clara Copperfield, sat by the fire, her face flushed from sobbing. "To think," she said to Peggotty, her maid, "that my poor baby will be born fatherless. And maybe motherless too. Who knows if I will survive the birth?"

"Nonsense," said Peggotty, handing my mother a steaming cup of tea. "Now don't you fret, Mrs. Copperfield. You have me to look after you."

My mother looked up with a slight smile, but then let out a yelp of surprise and hid behind her chair.

"What is it?" cried Peggotty.

My mother could only point. A fierce old lady had her nose pressed flat against the window. "Oh!" she said. "It must be Miss Betsey Trotwood. My husband's aunt. I recognize her from her picture."

The next moment, Miss Betsey strode through the door and looked slowly around the room. "Mrs. David Copperfield, I think?" she said at last, taking in my mother's mourning clothes.

"Yes," said my mother, faintly.

"Take off your cap, child," Miss Trotwood went on, "so I can see you."

My mother obediently removed her cap so that her golden curls came tumbling out.

"Tut, tut, tut," said Miss Trotwood. "You're nothing but a baby, and soon to have a babe of your own."

My mother hung her head and sobbed, as if her youth were all her fault.

"Don't cry, silly girl. Listen. Your baby will be a girl. Call her Betsey Trotwood after me and I'll be her godmother and best friend."

"But... what if it's not a..."

"Don't contradict," said Miss Trotwood. "I have a hunch, and they're always right."

Before midnight that night, Peggotty was running for the doctor. "Clara's time has come!" she told him. "Hurry!"

Miss Trotwood waited downstairs, pacing the floor. "How is she?" she demanded of the doctor, as soon as the new baby's cry wailed through the house.

"Mrs. Copperfield is well," replied the doctor.

"No, she... SHE, the baby!" barked Miss Trotwood impatiently.

"Madam, the baby is a boy," the doctor returned.

Miss Trotwood instantly walked out of the house and never came back.

That baby was me: David Copperfield. We – my mother, Peggotty and I – lived in our snug little cottage, which had a garden brimming with flowers and butterflies. Our fruit bushes had berries bigger and riper than any I've seen since; our apples, firm, red and round, were just like Peggotty's rosy cheeks.

David Copperfield

In winter we sat in the sitting room,
where a blazing log fire lit up my mother's
prettiness as I read aloud my books to her.
I loved my crocodile book most, with its
terrifying pictures. My home, in contrast, was
utterly safe.

When I was eight, a man named Mr. Murdstone began to visit our house. He had dark hair and strange eyes, so blank that you couldn't guess his thoughts. I saw how his attention made my mother smile.

At first he flattered me. "Come for a walk – just us, David," he invited.

We went to a hotel where his friends were staying: loud-voiced men, smoking cigars whose fumes made a stale stench in the room. They sprawled in armchairs, surrounded by half-empty bottles of wine.

"A toast for Mr. Murdstone!" they cried, pouring me a glass. "Drink to 'Success with the bewitching little widow!'"

"What does that mean?" I asked, sipping the wine.

They roared with laughter.

"Another toast!" they spluttered. "Propose it, David. Say: 'Confusion to young Mr. Copperfield.'"

"What do you mean?" I asked.

They found this even funnier. I knew they were laughing at me, but I was too young to understand why.

I saw Mr. Murdstone was at the root of it. Silent among his friends, I thought he looked evil. I wished my mother didn't like him.

"He'll leave us soon," I comforted myself. "Then Mother, Peggotty and I will be by ourselves again, snug and happy."

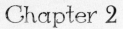

Chapter 2

Change

"Davy!" my mother said one day. "You and Peggotty are going to the seaside for a month, to visit her family. They live at Yarmouth."

"Lovely!" I jumped up and down excitedly. I'd never seen the sea.

Peggotty and I journeyed for miles by stagecoach.

"You'll love it in Yarmouth, Davy," she said. "You'll meet my brother, Daniel, and my nephew Ham. And there's his cousin, little Emily, same age as you."

The stagecoach stopped in a fishy smelling street and from there we walked to the beach.

"There's our house!" exclaimed Peggotty, wreathed in smiles.

I saw a black barge high and dry off the ground with a funnel sticking out of it for a chimney, smoking cheerfully. "That's not it?" I said. "That ship-looking thing?"

"That's it, Davy," said Peggotty.

She opened a little door cut into the side of the barge. Inside it was half ship, half house, and therein lay its magic. It had porthole windows, tiny furniture, and such a strong fish smell I felt I was being hugged by a lobster.

"I'm a fisherman," explained Peggotty's brother, Daniel. "'Course it smells of fish. Nice and fresh."

"C'mon, Davy," said Ham, kindly, as I hung back. "Let's go down to the beach." Off we trekked and little Emily came too. She was the prettiest girl I'd ever seen. We climbed the breakwater as the tide came in.

"Where's your mother?" I asked Emily.

"She's dead," Emily replied mournfully.

"My father's dead too. We're the same," I replied.

"No…" Emily disagreed, dancing dangerously on the narrow ledge above the roaring sea.

"I'm a fisherman's daughter, and you're a young gentleman. I want to be a fine lady," she added. "You have a much better time."

We played every day until the month was up. Going back home I was quiet, thinking of the seaside and the fun I'd had. I felt a little lonely; I wanted my mother and planned to rush into her arms.

Peggotty was unusually silent too, pressing her lips tight shut until she had her hand on our front door knob, ready to open it.

"I didn't like to tell you before, Davy," she confessed, "but you have a new Pa."

I shivered, guessing immediately it was Mr. Murdstone.

"Run in and say hello," Peggotty urged.

I did so, quaking with every step. On one side of the fire my mother sat sewing; on the other was Mr. Murdstone. My mother rose and opened her arms wide.

"Don't pamper him, Clara," said Mr. Murdstone. "Control yourself."

Instantly my mother sat down and went on sewing.

I felt as though an earthquake had ripped the ground from my feet. She loved Mr. Murdstone more than me! Nothing would ever be the same again.

I dashed upstairs and flung myself on my bed. Violent footsteps thumped up the stairs after me.

"You've upset your mother," hissed Mr. Murdstone as he flung open my door. "Bad boy! If I have a bad horse or dog, what do you think I do?"

"I don't know," I whispered.

"I thrash him. I say to myself, 'I'll conquer that animal if it costs him all the blood he has.' Now come downstairs to supper."

I obeyed. He was so threatening that I was
really scared. Yet if he'd said one word of
comfort, or welcome, or reassurance that home
was still home, I would have tried to like him.

I wondered why my mother didn't defend
me. I understood, later. Now they were
married, she understood his true nature. She
was afraid of him. Very afraid.

Chapter 3

I fall into disgrace

I'd never been to school. My mother gave me lessons at home, and I learned quickly and easily – until now.

"I'll teach David," Mr. Murdstone said. "It's time he had some discipline."

Under his glare, I forgot everything I knew... words swam before my eyes.

After a few weeks, he banged his fist on the table.

"You are STUPID!" he yelled.

"I'm not!" I contradicted defiantly.

"Then you're lazy and obstinate." He swished his cane to and fro. "You must be more careful today," he announced. "I'm going to test you on mental arithmetic."

I was so mesmerized by that swinging cane, I answered every question wrong.

Now he was binding the end of the cane with wire. "He must be beaten," snarled Mr. Murdstone. "I was beaten myself as a boy, and it did me no harm."

"Did it do you any good?" faltered my mother, bravely.

"How dare you, Clara!" he thundered.

My mother ran up to him, clinging onto his arm.

"You're a fool, Clara!" he said.

My mother covered her ears and I heard her crying. Then, holding his cane, Mr. Murdstone pulled me up to my room, and twisted my head under his arm.

"Please don't beat me!" I implored. "I can't learn with you. I just can't!"

"Really?" he mocked.

THWACK! He swiped me hard. In response I caught his hand between my teeth and bit it as hard as I could.

He flogged me furiously. I yelled and shrieked and so did he. My mother and Peggotty raced upstairs. He pushed them away and locked the door behind him, leaving me lying alone on the floor, filled with pain and anger.

I was a prisoner for five days. On the last night I woke to hear Peggotty whispering my name through the keyhole.

"Davy! They're sending you away to school tomorrow."

"School!" I was startled. "W-where?"

"Far away. Near London. Don't worry; you'll be happier away from him. I haven't come before because he wouldn't let me. But I've never stopped thinking about you. I'll hide a cake for you in the cart for the journey. Look under the door, now."

She pushed through some coins. Then she kissed the keyhole on her side of the door since she couldn't kiss me, and I, kneeling, kissed the keyhole my side too.

The feeling I had for Peggotty is hard to explain. She didn't replace my mother; no one could do that, but I felt a love for her that I've never had for anyone else.

The next day I said goodbye to my mother. She looked pale and miserable. "You disappoint me, Davy," she said, coldly. "You must control your temper." Mr. Murdstone had persuaded her that I was bad, and she believed him. That, to me, was his worst crime.

Chapter 4

School jungle

I climbed into the cart beside Mr. Barkis, the carrier man who was to drive me to school. Homesickness swept over me, and Mr. Barkis spread my tear-sodden hankie over his horse's back to dry.

"Hungry?" asked Mr. Barkis, eventually. "Peggotty, she said her name was – put in a cake for you."

"Yes!" I exclaimed eagerly. We shared it; Mr. Barkis was much struck by its taste.

"Never had such a good cake. What's her other cooking like? Pies? Pastry?..."

"Delicious," I replied.

He grunted thoughtfully. "Married, is she?...
Or in love?"

"I don't think so."

"Well then, I'll drop her the word. Barkis
is willing."

"You mean – you want to marry her?"

"That's right. If she wants to leave her job,
Barkis is willing."

"I hope you'll be happy," I said politely.
Privately, I prayed that Peggotty would
never leave my mother alone with cruel
Mr. Murdstone.

Two days later, we finally arrived. I said goodbye to Mr. Barkis who seemed like my last friend and met Mr. Creakle, the headmaster. His face was not reassuring – fiery red and bulging with purple veins.

"Here's your classroom, Copperfield," boomed Mr. Creakle. It was a long room bristling with rows of inky desks. It smelled like rotten apples mixed with mildewed books. On my own desk was a piece of paper, inscribed:

Beware. He bites.

"Where's the dog, Sir?" I asked, looking around.

"No dog, Copperfield," he said, tying the notice to my back. "Only yourself."

"Oh, Sir," I begged, appalled. "Please don't. The other boys will tease me…"

"Your stepfather ordered it," Mr. Creakle said. "I am a determined man, Copperfield. You will wear that notice."

Then he left me. I shrank against the wall, hiding my back, as the entire class swarmed in.

"Turn around, new boy," they chanted, twisting me in circles. "Show us what's on your back." It was like a nightmare.

"Stop!" ordered one boy, tall and handsome, with a friendly, easy manner. He was obviously popular because the other boys obeyed at once.

"I'm Steerforth," he said to me. "I hear you bit your stepfather."

I nodded. He looked me over and I looked up at him. "I expect he deserved it," he said at last, with a smile. Steerforth had saved me from the bullies. From that moment on, he was my hero.

"Got any money?" he asked.

"Seven shillings."

"Would you like a midnight feast? Do you like biscuits? Nuts?"

"Yes!" I said.

"Currant wine? Almond cake?"

"I like it all!" I replied.

"You shall have it," Steerforth said, kindly. "Just hand over the money."

That night, in the dormitory, Steerforth laid a sumptuous feast on my bed. "There you are! I'll share it with the other boys."

He did so, very fairly. Thus my popularity was ensured, but Peggotty's gift was all gone.

When I went home for the holidays, my mother held out a new baby.

"This is your brother, Davy. He looks just like you," she smiled, putting the white bundle in my arms.

"How dare you compare my son with yours?" Mr. Murdstone sneered. "Now, remember what you have to tell David."

My mother looked at me, her face pinched and white. "You can't stay with us here, Davy," she whispered. "You're to go to Yarmouth with Peggotty, until your term starts."

Peggotty and I left with some relief. My mother stood by the door, holding her baby, waving. That is how I think of her still, looking at me intently, and saying goodbye.

Chapter 5

A memorable birthday

Next term I had my ninth birthday. I was hoping for a letter from home, so I wasn't surprised when Mr. Creakle called me into his study.

"A visitor, Copperfield," he announced. I instantly thought my mother or Peggotty had come to see me...

It was Mr. Murdstone, his black eyes more inscrutable than ever.

"Your mother has died," he announced abruptly.

I was too stunned to think. Dead! I told myself, trying to take it in. Dead...

"The baby...?" I stammered.

"Fading fast," he said coldly. "Not expected to last the week. I'm not responsible for you now, though. I've come to tell you that you must leave school and earn your living."

"I can't do much," I gulped.

"Sulky as ever," he jeered. "I've found you a job in a factory, in London. Think yourself lucky. You'll live with a friend of a friend, Mr. Micawber, and pay him rent. Here's the address. Get packed and go."

"W-where's P-Peggotty?"

"Dismissed," he snapped, and was gone.

In a haze of misery, I went to get my things. I had to do as he said – there was no choice.

I had no money and no home. I wasn't even going to have an education. I knew that without it, Mr. Murdstone robbed me of my chance to make something of my life. I was driven to London, to Mr. Micawber's address, a house in a run-down back street.

A woman, clasping a screaming twin – the other was yelling on the floor – opened the door. "Come in!" she whispered. "Quick. Don't let the debt collector see you. He's always skulking about, waiting for a chance to get in. Not that there's money here, or anything else."

Slipping inside, I saw the sitting-room had no furniture at all.

"I'm Mrs. Micawber," she introduced herself. "You and your rent are welcome! Poor Mr. Micawber has been very unfortunate in his finances. But I'll never desert him. Never! The father of my twins, the husband of my heart."

Mr. Micawber now appeared, in floods of tears. "My angel," he sobbed. "Thank you."

I stared around the empty room.

"Yes, everything's gone," Mrs. Micawber confided. "Even my pearl necklace and my bracelets, all sold to pay our debts. But Mr. Micawber is a man of great talent. He just needs a chance."

"I'll give you some advice," said Mr. Micawber. "If only I'd taken it myself! Income twenty pounds, expenditure nineteen pounds: result happiness. Income twenty pounds, expenditure twenty-one pounds: result misery. But something will turn up," he continued, now beaming all over his face. "I'm hopeful."

Footsteps echoed in the street and we heard banging on the door.

"Pay your debts! Open up!" an angry voice called out.

"The door is locked," hissed Mrs. Micawber.

"The blossom is blighted," Mr. Micawber said, miserable again, his head in his hands. "As am I. The day sinks into unhappy night."

"I wish I could help," I said.

"You will," said Mrs. Micawber. "With your rent. Until then the cupboard is almost bare. There's hardly any supper."

We dined on stale cheese and cider, which made Mr. Micawber feel better.

"Something will certainly turn up soon," he said, waving his glass. "Let's sing a little song," and he began to warble, "*Gee up, Dobbin! Gee ho, Dobbin! Gee up, Dobbin! Gee up, and Gee Ho-o-o!*" until Mrs. Micawber declared it was time for bed.

The next day I began work in a warehouse, full of glass bottles. My job was to rinse them, hold them up to the light to check for cracks, stick labels on the full ones and cork them.

Day in, day out I worked alone, crushed with secret agony. I was ashamed of my position. I thought of Steerforth and my school friends. They had a future; I did not. I thought of my mother – gone, like a dream that ends in the cold light of dawn.

Chapter 6

Aunt Betsey

"It is time for us to say farewell," Mrs. Micawber informed me one day. "Mr. Micawber and I are leaving London."

"Where are you going?" I asked.

"To Plymouth. My family thinks Mr. Micawber will do better outside London. And I shall go with him. He is the parent of my children, father of my twins. I shall never desert Mr. Micawber."

302

I said goodbye to both of them and there were many tears at our parting.

"I shall never forget you," said Mrs. Micawber. "You have never been a lodger. You have been a friend."

Once the Micawbers had left, I went to begin my day at the factory. But already I had decided not to pass many more weary days there. I'd had enough. I was going to run away.

I remembered Peggotty telling me about my aunt, Miss Betsey Trotwood, who had stormed out of the house the night I was born. Perhaps she would help me.

I didn't know where Peggotty was, but I wrote to the barge house in Yarmouth in case her family knew. Back came a letter from Peggotty herself.

Dear Davy,

How wonderful to hear from my boy. I've been wondering so much where you were, and that horrible Murdstone man wouldn't tell me. Your Aunt lives somewhere in Dover. Can you get there? If not, come here. I am married to Barkis, and am very happy. Emily sends her love and so do I.

Peggotty Barkis

I had no money, though. I found a pawn shop and exchanged my jacket and hat for my fare out of London. After that I walked... for days. I was soon exhausted. My feet grew sore with blisters and my stomach ached with hunger.

One black night, huddled in a hedge, I opened my eyes in terror. A beggar shook me awake. I smelled his beery breath.

"Got any money?" he growled.

"N-no..."

"Then give me yer silk hanky. And yer shoes."

With an ugly laugh he tore them off as I wriggled away and escaped into the shadows. I was miserable, filthy, ragged and barefoot. Only the thought of finding Aunt Betsey kept me going.

At last I reached Dover. I asked everywhere
for Miss Trotwood's house, and was
directed to a neat little cottage.
Opening the gate, I saw a
lady clipping a hedge
with garden shears.

"Go away," she called, waving them at me. "No beggars here."

"Please, Aunt..." I began.

"Good Lord! Who are you?"

"I'm your nephew, David Copperfield." I told her everything. When I had finished, Aunt Betsey sighed.

"I believe you. Your mother was a weak, foolish child, but she had a loving heart, and that wicked man as good as murdered her with unkindness. I should have kept an eye on her. I'll adopt you."

"Thank you," I gasped.

"That's my way of making amends. We'll visit my lawyer, Mr. Wickfield, tomorrow. I want it legally watertight, so that Murdstone can never claim you. What you need now is food, a hot bath and new clothes. I'll call you Trot," she added.

My aunt was quick and abrupt, but I felt I could trust her. I knew I'd come home.

The next day we went to Mr. Wickfield's
office. A bony, pale, red-haired man showed
us in.

"This is Uriah Heep, Mr. Wickfield's clerk,"
said my aunt. "My nephew: David Trotwood
Copperfield."

Uriah extended a cold, damp hand, and I
secretly wiped my hand behind my back to get
rid of his clammy feel.

"I want to see Mr. Wickfield," Aunt Betsey
demanded.

"Yes, madam, I'll find him, madam. I wouldn't dream of keeping you waiting. I'm humble. I know my place." He rubbed his palms together, cringingly.

"Hurry," my aunt ordered, waving her fist impatiently.

Uriah slunk off, disappearing down the corridor like a thin, white worm. "Thank you for your attention, Miss Trotwood. I've much to be thankful for," we heard him say.

My aunt explained her business to Mr. Wickfield. "I want an excellent school for him," she concluded.

Mr. Wickfield stroked his chin thoughtfully. "The best one is almost full. He'll need somewhere to board. He can live here, with my little housekeeper and myself. Here she is."

He opened a door to a room full of books and flowers, where sunlight sparkled through diamond panes onto glorious oak beams and bright furniture. By a merrily crackling fire was a girl my own age, sorting household bills.

"My daughter, Agnes," said Mr. Wickfield. "Since her mother died, she's run this house."

Agnes smiled at me. She looked so serene and sweet that afterwards, whenever I saw sunshine lighting up a room, I thought of her.

"He can start next week," my aunt announced. "Now Trot," she continued, "be a credit to yourself and to me. Never be mean, never be false, never be cruel."

Her words – and her kindness – inspired me.

"I won't forget," I vowed. "I'll always do my best."

Chapter 7

Ten years later

Time, silent and gliding, creeps up on me. Once I was the new boy, then, before I knew it, I was head boy, top of the school, looking down on the line of new boys below me.

What other changes have come upon me? I wear a gold watch and chain, and a long-tailed coat. I'm training to be a lawyer, with Mr. Wickfield's friend, Mr. Spenlow. I have also started to publish magazine articles. To my delight, I am becoming well known as a writer.

And what of the little girl I saw on my first day at Mr. Wicklow's? She is gone. In her place, the woman I think of as my sweet sister – Agnes, to whom I tell everything. I confide that I am in love with Mr. Spenlow's daughter, Dora. She is divinely pretty, like a perfect doll, and so tender with her little dog, Jip. Being in love with Dora is like being in Fairyland. I am steeped in love for her. The sun shines Dora, and the birds sing Dora. It is all Dora to me.

Before I knew it, I had declared my love for her and asked her to be my wife.

"I'd love to marry you," Dora sighed, blushing adorably.

"We won't be rich, I'm afraid," I said. "I'll have to work very hard."

"Don't talk like that. It's so unpleasant," she said, nestling closer, petting her dog. "Although Jip must have his lamb chop every day or he'll die."

She looked so tiny and sweet that I kissed her. As soon as it could be arranged, we married. And after the honeymoon, we came back to our new little home.

"What's for supper?" I asked hopefully the first night, after work.

Dora looked startled. "Nothing! I forgot. I was playing with Jip."

"We'll go out," I said. "It doesn't matter at all."

Night after night Dora forgot, or cooked something unrecognizable and disgusting.

We laughed about it, though I could tell she wasn't proud of herself.

"Don't scold me," she wept. "You're disappointed. I can't housekeep. I'm too silly – not like you – becoming more famous every minute with your writing."

"I love you just as you are," I said, resolving to do more than my share to help her.

Aunt Betsey saw our difficulties. "Be patient, Trot. She's a fragile girl," she warned me.

Agnes stayed with us a lot. "Dora is so lovely," she told me. "Like a fairy princess." Agnes's sweetness made the whole house shine brighter and Dora and I both felt better for her calming presence.

Aunt Betsey was right. Dora was delicate. She fell ill before we'd been married a year and grew steadily weaker.

"I'm not going to get better," she told me faintly as I sat by her bedside. "Don't be unhappy – it's better this way. I was too young for you. I was your child-wife. You'd have grown tired of me."

"Never... Never!" I cried, holding her frail body tight in my arms.

Soon after that, my poor Dora died.

I went abroad to Switzerland, for a year, then two, living alone and writing, trying to escape from my unhappiness. From there, I wrote to Peggotty. In my sorrow, I was filled with longing to see her again.

She was overjoyed to hear from me, and begged me to come to Yarmouth, where she was living. I decided I had been alone for long enough, and set out for England, and the barge house where I had once been so happy.

Marriage suited Peggotty. Her cheeks were

rounder and redder than ever. She spoiled me with devotion, plying me with home-cooked food.

But much had changed. Emily had gone, her nephew Ham, and Daniel too.

"Emily was engaged to Ham," Peggotty told me. "He doted on her, treating her like the timid little bird she was. But a fine young gentleman came to town, and she upped and went away with him. Emily always wanted to be a fine young lady."

"What happened then?" I asked.

"Daniel went after her. We all knew that gentleman meant no good by her. He was just going to drop Emily when he tired of her – and Daniel wanted to be there when that happened, to make sure she didn't come to any harm."

Peggotty was silent for a moment, staring at the flames in the old hearth. "Ham was never the same after that. He was still as gentle as he ever was – but he'd lost all heart.

"And then one day, there was a great storm at sea, and a ship, caught in the thick of it. No one else would brave the waters, but Ham dashed into the sea again and again, saving as many as he could. Then he went in one last time – right into the foaming waves – and never came out again."

"And who was he?" I asked, filled with rage at the thought of him. "This man who stole Emily from her home?"

"It was Steerforth," Peggotty said. "The friend you wrote about from school. For your sake, we made him welcome here."

"Steerforth?" I cried. In one stroke, I mourned the loss of Ham, of Emily's happiness – and my childhood hero, gone forever. I understood his true nature now. He was full of charm, but ruthless too.

I stayed with Peggotty for many months. In her loving presence, I felt my heart begin to heal. And, every day, I wrote to Agnes. She was so good to me. As I read her letters, I felt her sweet, tranquil nature calm me. Until, at last, I was ready to return to my old life once again.

As soon as I arrived, my Aunt whisked me off to Mr. Wickfield's. "There's been strange goings-on since you left," she told me. "And it must stop."

I found Mr. Wickfield much changed. His face looked haggard and his hands shook when I greeted him. Uriah Heep was always at his side, pouring him glass after glass of whisky.

"I understand what you're doing, Uriah," I said, anger clearing my mind. "You've made the old man depend on you, and alcohol, until he's lost his mind."

"Yes!" Uriah simpered. "I'm master here now. Why should I be humble all my life? I'm going to marry Agnes. She'll find she has no choice. Her father's lost his fortune – to me!"

"You fiend, Uriah!" I shouted. The thought of Agnes and Uriah together sickened me.

Suddenly I knew, as clear as light, that no one must marry Agnes, but me. I'd never forget Dora, my sweet child-wife, but I loved Agnes. I always had.

I came upon her in the bookroom, where she was reading alone by the fire. She turned her pale face to mine.

"Dearest Agnes," I said, then stopped. Was it selfish to say more? But I couldn't believe she loved Uriah. "You have always been like a sister to me. But now I long to call you something more than sister – something very different."

I saw her face glow with pleasure.

Her tears fell fast, but they were not tears of sorrow, and I felt my hope brighten in them.

"I loved Dora," I said, "but even then, my love would have been incomplete without your sympathy. And when I lost her, Agnes, I couldn't have gone on without the thought of you."

"There is just one thing I must tell you," Agnes whispered.

"What is it?" I asked.

She gently laid her hands upon my shoulders, and looked calmly up at my face. "I have loved you all my life."

I held her in my arms and felt my eyes fill with tears of pure joy.

Afterword

And now my written story ends. I remember the boy I once was, happy with my mother, then cast out and quite alone. I see the faces of my family and friends, but as I close my task these faces fade away and I see myself, with Agnes at my side, journeying along the road of life. My lamp burns low; I have written far into the night. It is time for me to go...

This picture shows David Copperfield writing
his story, but it could as easily be Charles Dickens.
The novel "David Copperfield" was the
closest to Dickens' own life.

The Life and Times of Charles Dickens

Charles Dickens
1812–1870

Charles Dickens was born in Portsea (now Portsmouth), England on February 7, 1812. His father, John Dickens, was a clerk in the Navy and he was the second of eight children.

John Dickens and Elizabeth, his wife

Early childhood

When Dickens was five, the family moved to Chatham in Kent and he spent several very happy years going to school, playing and exploring the surrounding countryside.

One day, he was out on a walk with his father, when he saw the grand house, Gad's Hill Place.

Gad's Hill Place

Charles was entranced.

"If you work hard enough," said John Dickens, "one day you might live there."

But in 1822, his father moved them all from Kent to London. The Dickens family – by then, John and his wife Elizabeth, Charles and four other children, plus a servant and a lodger – all squashed into a tiny cottage in Camden Town, London.

It was the start of a dramatic change, which was to affect Dickens' life and his writing career.

Disaster strikes

Mr. Micawber and family

Dickens' father was a sociable man who loved entertaining, but he had no head for figures and spent far more than he earned. It was to lead the family into trouble – and inspired the character Mr. Micawber in *David Copperfield.*

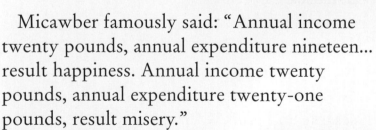

Micawber famously said: "Annual income twenty pounds, annual expenditure nineteen... result happiness. Annual income twenty pounds, annual expenditure twenty-one pounds, result misery."

The family had no money to spare so, aged just ten, Dickens was taken out of school. Not long after that he was sent to work.

He spent all day trimming and sticking labels on pots of blacking (shoe polish) at Warren's Blacking Warehouse. On his first day, a boy named Bob Fagin showed him what to do. Dickens never forgot him and, over a decade later, his name appeared in *Oliver Twist*.

Finally, John Dickens owed so much money, he was sent to a debtor's prison – the Victorian answer for those who couldn't pay their debts. The rest of the family moved into Marshalsea Debtors' Prison with John, while Charles found lodgings in the city's slums.

Dickens was utterly miserable and completely humiliated, but every slum he walked through, every person he met, even the

Sticking labels on pots of blacking

prison itself were stored in his memory and later used in his books. *Oliver Twist* seethes with the terrible things done to children and the poor. And in his novel *Little Dorrit*, the heroine Amy is born and grows up in the Marshalsea Prison.

Luckily, John Dickens inherited some money. He was able to pay his debts and left the prison, reuniting the family and allowing Charles to go back to school for another three years.

Early writing

At fifteen, Dickens went to work in a lawyer's office, where the main thing he learned was to loathe the law and lawyers. This comes out strongly in his novel *Bleak House*,

where the fictional case of *Jarndyce and Jarndyce* rambles on for generations, as the greedy lawyers use up all the money. In *Oliver Twist*, Mr. Bumble even declares the law to be an idiot.

Not happy as a clerk, Dickens became a legal journalist. Between 1833 and 1835, he went all over the country, reporting cases.

A courtroom scene from Bleak House

At the same time, he was writing short stories and articles for magazines. In 1834, he invented the pen name Boz and published *Sketches by Boz*, full of his observations of the Victorian world.

Dickens at 18

Editor and writer

When Dickens started writing, popular novels often came in parts, printed weekly or monthly in magazines. They were the soap operas of their day. Each chapter ended on a cliffhanger, leaving readers desperate for the next one.

In 1836, part one of Dickens' first novel, *The Posthumous Papers of the Pickwick Club*

Samuel Pickwick, hero of The Pickwick Papers

(or *The Pickwick Papers*) was published. Within a few months everyone was talking about him.

Soon, he was writing feverishly. In the next couple of years, he wrote both *Oliver Twist* and *Nicholas Nickleby* in monthly instalments, barely keeping up with his readers' demands for more.

In 1840, his next novel, *The Old Curiosity Shop* started to appear in weekly parts in a magazine named *Master Humphrey's Clock*. The setting was inspired by a London shop that is still open for customers today.

The Old Curiosity Shop, in Portsmouth Street, London

The story was so popular, the magazine sold more than 100,000 copies a week. People would come up to Dickens in the street and beg him not to kill off his heroine, Little Nell.

His stories and fame quickly spread abroad. There is even a tale that people in America were so anxious to know what happened to Little Nell, they thronged the docks, calling out to people as they got off boats from Europe, asking whether Little Nell lived or died.

Alongside his novels, Dickens edited various magazines. In 1850, he founded his own journal, *Household Words*, which published his novels and gave him a chance to communicate to his readers through articles.

Charles Dickens wrote all of his novels and articles by hand, either with a quill or pen and ink.

Life in Victorian London

Dickens spent days and nights walking around London, collecting material for his books. London ~ violent, dirty and yet stunningly beautiful in places ~ was a city of huge contrasts. The biggest contrast of all was between the wealthy, with their huge houses, leisured lives and servants, and those who were desperately poor.

The poorest faced being sent to the dreaded workhouse, where families were split up. They worked long hours, lived in crowded and dirty quarters and were barely given enough to eat. Dickens showed this dramatically in an early scene in *Oliver Twist*, when Oliver dares to ask for more gruel.

Oliver asking for more

Dickens' novels were full of the social horrors he saw around him but he wasn't content to simply show his readers, through books and articles, the appalling state of the society in which they lived.

Charles Dickens at 40

He also gave passionate speeches calling for change. Dickens spoke to all kinds of groups, criticizing the Poor Law (which had introduced workhouses); the terrible things that happened to unwanted children; and the corruption that infected the highest levels of government and the law.

Where the poorest children were concerned, speeches were not enough. Dickens was horrified that slum children had to turn to crime to survive. He was convinced that education could help them to a better life. But this was a time when all schooling had to be paid for. So he donated money to the Ragged Schools Movement, set up to teach inner-city children for free (and named after the pupils in their ragged clothing).

Oliver Twist and Dodger walking through
a street in one of London's slums

Family and friends

When Dickens was still a law reporter he fell in love with a pretty young woman named Maria Beadnell. She saw him for a while but, when he confessed his feelings, she rejected him. Many years later, they met again. Maria had not aged well and Dickens took his revenge by basing a character on her. Flora Finching in *Little Dorrit* is enchanting at first, but grows silly and extremely unattractive.

In 1834, the year after Maria refused him, Dickens met Catherine Hogarth and in 1836, they were married. Over the next 16 years they had ten children: Charley, Mary, Kate, Walter, Francis, Alfred, Sydney, Harry, Dora and Edward.

Catherine Dickens née Hogarth

Shortly after Dickens' marriage to Catherine, her sixteen-year-old sister, Mary, moved in with them. Charles grew very fond of Mary, forming a close friendship with her.

Then, one night after a trip to see a play, Mary complained of feeling unwell. She died the next day, aged just seventeen.

Mary Hogarth

Dickens was so upset, he was unable to write the current instalment of *The Pickwick Papers*, one of the few times a serial was ever interrupted. Mary's sudden death was subsequently immortalized in *The Old Curiosity Shop*, where the young heroine meets a tragic end.

Georgina Hogarth

Another of Catherine's sisters, Georgina, joined the family in 1842 and took over running the household. Dickens was soon relying on both Georgina's housekeeping skills and her friendship. Catherine and Dickens gradually grew apart, finally separating in 1858. But Georgina stayed with Dickens to run his recently bought home, the house he had admired as a boy: Gad's Hill Place.

Dickens' companion after he left his wife was a young actress named Ellen Ternan. The pair had met when acting in a play together.

Ellen Ternan

Dickens the actor

Dickens loved the stage. In his novel, *Nicholas Nickleby*, the hero joins an acting comany, writing a play for them and taking a lead role.

Dickens himself was a frequent play-goer, but he also acted in and produced many amateur productions, even performing for Queen Victoria. One of his most popular performances was as Captain Bobadil, an old soldier, in a 16th-century play by Ben Jonson.

Dickens in costume as
Captain Bobadil

Reading and America

Dickens loved acting so much that, in 1858, he began to give dramatized readings of his books. He went all over Europe and North America, delighting audiences.

On Dickens' first trip to America, he had annoyed many people by speaking out against everything from spitting in the street to slavery. He also resented the fact that he wasn't paid for American editions of his books. He was so disappointed, in fact, that he was rude about America in his novel *Martin Chuzzlewit*.

This put Americans off him for quite some time. But by the time of his reading tours, they had forgiven him.

Dickens giving a reading

The Christmas Stories

In 1843, Dickens began a series of books celebrating Christmas. At the time, Europe was in the grip of a mini-Ice Age. Winters were so cold that rivers froze and snow lay thick upon the ground. Dickens' Christmas stories are full of picturesque snowy scenes, which is why we have an image of snowy Christmases today.

The most famous story of all is *A Christmas Carol*, the tale of a miser named Scrooge, whose heart is as cold as the snow outside. Over just one night, Scrooge is taken on a life-changing journey through past, present and future by three unforgettable ghosts.

Scrooge sees the ghost of his old friend Marley

Last days

As Dickens grew older, he worked harder than ever with his writing and journalism and readings.

When he wasn't touring, he would retire to the summer house in the garden of Gad's Hill Place and write. Here he wrote *A Tale of Two Cities*, *Great Expectations* and *Our Mutual Friend*.

But the demanding tours and constant writing took its toll. Despite being exhausted, he kept driving himself to work harder.

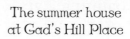

The summer house at Gad's Hill Place

On June 8, 1870, having spent the day in his summer house working on his latest novel, *The Mystery of Edwin Drood*, he was taken ill at the dinner table. He died the next day and was buried in Poet's Corner at Westminster Abbey, in London.

The inscription on Dickens' tomb is a simple one:

CHARLES DICKENS
BORN 7TH FEBRUARY 1812
DIED 9TH JUNE 1870

He had asked for the plainest inscription and hoped that people might remember him through his books. His wish came true. His books have been adapted into plays, films, television series and even smash-hit musicals, all painting a vivid picture of Victorian London, and filled with larger-than-life characters who leap off the page.

Bibliography

1836	*Collected Sketches by Boz*
1836-7	*The Posthumous Papers of the Pickwick Club*
1837-9	*Oliver Twist* *Nicholas Nickleby*
1840-1	*The Old Curiosity Shop* *Barnaby Rudge*
1843	*A Christmas Carol* (*Christmas Books series*)
1843-4	*Martin Chuzzlewit*
1844	*The Chimes* (*Christmas Books series*)
1845	*The Cricket on the Hearth* (*Christmas Books series*)

1846	*The Battle of Life* (*Christmas Books series*)
1846-8	*Dombey and Son*
1848	*The Haunted Man* (*Christmas Books series*)
1849-50	*David Copperfield*
1852-3	*Bleak House*
1854	*Hard Times*
1855-7	*Little Dorrit*
1859	*A Tale of Two Cities*
1860-1	*Great Expectations*
1864-5	*Our Mutual Friend*
1870	*The Mystery of Edwin Drood* (unfinished)

Usborne Quicklinks

For links to websites where you can find out more about Charles Dickens, his novels and life in Victorian times, go to the Usborne Quicklinks Website at www.usborne-quicklinks.com and type in the keywords "Charles Dickens".

Here are some of the things you can do at the recommended websites:

* Take a tour of Victorian London.

* Watch short clips from films of Dickens' novels.

* Find out more about Dickens' memorable characters.

* See animated movies about what life was like for Victorian children.

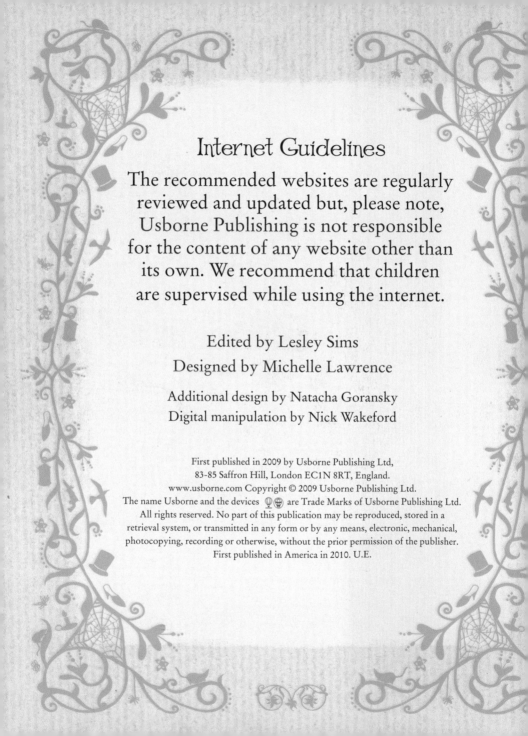

Internet Guidelines

The recommended websites are regularly reviewed and updated but, please note, Usborne Publishing is not responsible for the content of any website other than its own. We recommend that children are supervised while using the internet.

Edited by Lesley Sims
Designed by Michelle Lawrence

Additional design by Natacha Goransky
Digital manipulation by Nick Wakeford